NEW YORK REVIE
CLASSICS

THE FROG IN THE THROAT

MARKUS WERNER (1944–2016) was born in Eschlikon, Switzerland, and raised in the canton of Schaffhausen. He studied German language and literature at the University of Zurich, where he wrote a doctoral thesis on the work of Max Frisch. For most of the 1970s and '80s, he was a teacher—a profession from which he retired eagerly in 1990 to become a full-time writer. As he put it in a rare self-portrait: "I smoke, write haltingly, and live in the country." He wrote very haltingly, or rather meticulously indeed, publishing seven novels in the course of twenty years—among them *Zündel's Exit* (1984), *Cold Shoulder* (1989), and *On the Edge* (2004).

MICHAEL HOFMANN is a German-born, British-educated poet, critic, and translator. His most recent books are *One Lark, One Horse* (poems) and *Messing About in Boats* (essays). For New York Review Books he has translated several works, including Alfred Döblin's *Berlin Alexanderplatz*, and edited an anthology of writing by Malcolm Lowry, *The Voyage That Never Ends*. In 2024, his translation of Jenny Erpenbeck's novel *Kairos* won the International Booker Prize.

THE FROG IN THE THROAT

MARKUS WERNER

*Translated from the German and
with an introduction by*
MICHAEL HOFMANN

NEW YORK REVIEW BOOKS

New York

THIS IS A NEW YORK REVIEW BOOK
PUBLISHED BY THE NEW YORK REVIEW OF BOOKS
207 East 32nd Street, New York, NY 10016
www.nyrb.com

Originally published in the German language as *Froschnacht*.

Library of Congress Cataloging-in-Publication Data
Names: Werner, Markus, author. | Hofmann, Michael, 1957 August 25– translator.
Title: The frog in the throat / Markus Werner; translated from the German by
   Michael Hofmann.
Other titles: Froschnacht. English
Description: New York: New York Review Books, 2025. | Series: New York Review
   Books classics | Identifiers: LCCN 2024039875 (print) | LCCN 2024039876
   (ebook) | ISBN 9781681379128 (paperback) | ISBN 9781681379135 (ebook)
Subjects: LCGFT: Black humor. | Novels.
Classification: LCC PT2685.E6736 F7613 2025 (print) | LCC PT2685.E6736
   (ebook) | DDC 833/.914—dc23/eng/20240830
LC record available at https://lccn.loc.gov/2024039875
LC ebook record available at https://lccn.loc.gov/2024039876

ISBN 978-1-68137-912-8
Available as an electronic book; ISBN 978-1-68137-913-5

Printed in the United States of America on acid-free paper.
10 9 8 7 6 5 4 3 2 1

INTRODUCTION

THE SWISS author Markus Werner—beard, curls, grizzle, glasses, absence of affect, we corresponded but I never met him—was a cult writer at the turn of the millennium, the sort of writer whose books traveled by word of mouth among readers, a *Geheimtip* in the German *Sprachraum*. Yes, he had some qualified admirers (not in the sense of qualified admiration, but—you know), experienced and intelligent critics like Marcel Reich-Ranicki and Helmut Böttiger, and he won the odd prize, but his reputation was not one of those seeking to be imposed from above. Rather, Werner's name was passed around among grateful and slightly incredulous readers—incredulous that something could be this swift, this bleak, and this deadly.

Werner's literary production consisted of seven short, barbed novels published between 1984 and 2004, between his fortieth and his sixtieth year, beginning with *Zündels Abgang* and concluding with *Am Hang*. The latter was translated into English by Robert E. Goodwin as *On the Edge*; the first, as *Zündel's Exit*—and the third as well, *Cold Shoulder* (*Die kalte Schulter*)—by the present translator. For a private, quirky, and scandal-free foreign writer, retired from schoolmastering, then from authorship, and finally from the lists of the living, this would seem to be a respectable showing, three books. But here's the thing: If one has a taste for Werner, and not everyone does, one German reviewer actually pleaded with his readers *not to buy the book*, but if one does, one may well hold the author to be one of the glories of the contemporary—the recent—scene and find the product exquisitely addictive, and there are only seven of them, and why would one ever willingly stop?

Werner's books dramatize figures on the outs with life. There is a loose thread, which may be something distinctly trivial, often something written or said, a word or a phrase in a postcard or a newspaper or a telephone call, and the Werner figure (and these exist, just as the Bernhard figure exists, or the Kafka figure exists) tugs at it. Perhaps it's a communication cord, or a bell rope or a fuse. He—it's usually a "he"—pulls at it idly or experimentally, in a spirit of irritation or retaliation, vengeance or self-defense, and then, like the translator above, won't willingly stop. He becomes a verbal and attitudinal terrorist. A table setting sets him off not because it's wrong or he's fussy (though he is) but merely by being there the night before and presuming on a tomorrow with breakfast. He goes on picking and pulling. Existence very rapidly—in the space of a few score pages— loses its texture, its weft or its warp; shreds of it hang down looking unappealing and distinctly unlivable. Whole worlds or what had been worlds devolve to piles of lint: first, or most grievously, the innermost circle of the *Intimsphäre*, one's minimal domestic existence in what Randall Jarrell once called the "group of two," the home life or private life or emotional life that in Werner is always overpriced and over-privileged, the only "soft" or "premium" part of life, the desert island of feeling in a sea of verbiage and uncouthness and commerce. And then rapidly also one's professional life, one's wider setting and prospects, and finally the possibility of a continued conventional existence within language and society.

The novels seem to catch Werner's heroes (a doubtful term in his context) at bad moments: there has been a mishap involving a cigarette machine, an ill-timed absence, an unendurable professional humiliation. A provocation that could have been surmounted, perhaps even has been surmounted, nine times is unendurable a tenth. The books give a sense—true, I believe—of something not built into being but cut down into it. They cling fast to economy, a jaggedness of utterance, a scorn for platitude, a ruthless, look-no-brakes speed. They are the kind of books that Thalmann (in the present novel) favors, remarking "their authors, in writing them, did so to avoid doing something far worse." Whatever that may have been. Read enough of Werner's books, and you will come to an appreciation that life is just about made up of such "bad moments," one after another. And then? Then it's a question of attitude, of self-respect, of resistance, of what the French once called *contenance*. If you have ever wondered why you go on taking it (whatever "it" is), and what would happen if you maybe stopped, or if you work for Elon Musk, then Werner is for you.

Werner's books seem to touch opposites. Are they mono-dramas or about the condition of society? Specifically Swiss or all-purpose Western post–World War II? Are they concerned with toenails and turds, or mostly with our immortal souls? Are they couples-y or about solitary males? Timeless or niched in the 1980s? Doleful or exuberant? Political or post-political? Torpid or frantically energetic? Are their predicaments—as is sometimes debated with reference to Henrik Ibsen's plays—curable or not? Do they give heart or tell the reader to abandon all hope? Do they teach independence or reward conformism? Are they tragedies or comedies? Predictably, the answer to all is "yes" or "both."

That thing that W.H. Auden would first look for in a piece of writing, "the contraption," is abundantly there in Werner. Hair-triggered by a moment's mishap, they surge toward a seduction, a bid for escape, a resignation, a farcical attempt at suicide, a grill party with neighbors. Whatever is set up, the books deliver. They are fitted together like West End farces, miracles of timing, one door slamming just as another six—no, don't open, but slam shut at the same time. The character is adrift in their draft like a withered leaf. In the 1970s, we were just through being told that life was impossible. We were beginning to worry about ecology and overpopulation. There was a working class, but that went by "middle," or "lower middle," and it was threatened by the coming of automation and robots (which in another language means "work"). The word "society" had just been withdrawn and replaced in general use by the word "economy." Unions of all sorts were fallen into disrepute. Italy was rumored to have overtaken England; the US was in a long post-Vietnam trough; powered by first-wave feminism, women had without question surpassed men; and Switzerland was no longer chocolate and cheese, or even Swiss watches and cuckoo clocks, but frankly pharmaceuticals and financial jiggery-pokery. Television—the media—was proliferating, well, like frog spawn, and our overexposed rhetorics of persuasion and opinion and even of introspection were looking distinctly shopworn. It was the dusk of the Age of Respect. Terror of the Left and Terror of the Right—separately, mind you—had set up in opposition to the Terror of the Middle.

*

The Frog in the Throat (*Froschnacht*) was Werner's second novel, appearing in 1985, the year after *Zündel's Exit*. The death promised or suggested in the title of that book, has already happened in this one; it is that of the older Thalmann, Klemens by name though hardly by nature, who in some male parody of a period haunts his defrocked son Franz once a month for three days in the form of a frog in his throat and agonies of introversion and justification. The book covers the six months after Klemens Thalmann's death, and its ten chapters are five paired solo scenes: Franz, Klemens; Franz, Klemens; and so on. (This is the "contraption.") Franz struggles with his frog, soliloquizes through his somewhat shameful "anecdote-enriched past"; while Klemens, his head companionably pressed against the flanks of each of his five cows, talks to his now-preferred audience. It is a book about Switzerland and about the modern age, about the great leap forward out of a productive to a service economy (or what, in a further degeneration, we call the "knowledge economy")— Franz, having left the cloth and taken up the noble calling of life coach.

What is miraculous in such a short book is how Werner manages to make such a dense weave of existence. It is possible—in fact, I would urge it—to read *The Frog in the Throat* again and again, so deeply and subtly is so much information dissolved in it. With just a few strokes of the pen, the author gives us three highly individuated generations of Thalmanns across most of the twentieth century, men and women, parents and children; the long life of Klemens and his many village contacts, and the long midlife of Franz and a few of his many clients. Numerous tiny scenes sharply assert themselves: with Helen in the lewd Greek taxi, phoning Frau Trüssel in the passport office for some pointers, the landlady's ribald calls in the pub, Kezia's lakeside seduction moves, the respective quirks of five cows, the first Kennedy assassination.

Werner has an utterly distinctive way with a sentence, which in his practice is something brief but highly flavored and often studded with unexpected vocabulary, a kind of ideal labeling. Say, the syndrome that regularly befell Franz at the foot of the pulpit, that he calls "reverend's remorse" or "*taedium crucis*." What will remain of us is not whatever Larkin says, but maybe irony. Many of Werner's sentences are exquisitely dispirited, of which just one shall be let stand here: "We wandered silently in the general direction of Sparta." The book gives us births and deaths, a strong sense of a dwindling social horizon across the twentieth century; Klemens still political, still with his radio and his newspapers, and his socialist and global arguments; Franz seemingly not interested in anything beyond his job and his personal life, and the eventual realization of his aspiration, which is the completion of his switch from "worried Christ" to "carefree Buddha," in the apt terms of Wisława Szymborska:

> I promise you one thing, though: One day I'll be sitting under a grapevine, or maybe a fig tree. I'll draw deep and satisfying breaths through my shamelessly open mouth, and the sun will warm my tonsils, and no one will stop me. You'll be lying off to the side in the grass, still just about wiggling, but little more than a corpse.

The Frog in the Throat finds room for such recurring markers as the magical shrub the elderflower, or the graveyards (not uncommon in Werner)—the one in Fez, the site of all life and all joy; the one in the local town where Kezia plies her trade; and the one in the village with the intoxicating unapproved elderflower that Klemens planted over the grave of old Knüsel, his schoolteacher.

The two men, father and son, Thalmann and Thalmann, are at loggerheads, ten years broken, cut off, and set aside. They are opposites, the one who lived by the rules (or did he?) morally and mortally let down by his son who threw over the traces, the widower and the accidental Don Juan. In fact, the book shows us, they are not so much opponents— a crossed line of battle—as they are cussed, independent souls, lines in parallel destined to meet in infinity. Both quarrel with their lot, both see themselves as done down, both are full of resentment and unappeased aggression. They put me in mind of the ending of "Remembering My Father" by another great Polish poet, Zbigniew Herbert (translated by John and Bogdana Carpenter):

> he himself grows in me we eat our defeats
> we burst out laughing
> when they say how little is needed
> to be reconciled

Of course, reconciliation is out of the question, but equally there is no possibility of not laughing. Until infinity.

—MICHAEL HOFMANN
December 2022

THE FROG IN THE THROAT

I

He comes once a month, makes himself at home, stays for three days. In my throat, where else. Have you tried gargling, comes the well-meaning advice. Tried that, tried everything. Never less than three days.

Filthy effing frog.

The third night is always the worst. He knows he's on the way out. Loafs around, robs me of air and sleep. It's enough to drive a man to drink. I sit and swig and splutter and dream about how I've rescued lovely ladies from burning buildings, plugged the odd villain in the leg. Sometimes I'm lying in a hospital, all in white, so brave in my exemplary dying. I've been a little girl in my time, saw right through my eleven suitors, and sent them all packing.

I sit and scribble and muse, as I've learned to do at institutions of learning in Zurich and Cologne and Boston. No control, some control, let it go, let it go. Within me is the frog, within reach is a glass of rough red, and in front of me, oh woe!, the blank sheet of paper.

Thalmann's the name, Franz Thalmann, divorced these ten years. Hey, Franz, do you have a prehistory, then? I do, as long as my leg, maybe I'll tell you later. Now I'm forty-nine, and I was thrown off the scent by a scent, but as I say, more later.

Forty-nine, then. The body's diminished elasticity, can barely touch its toes, capacity for joy is mostly gone. Thalmann. Boozehound, ex-minister, subsequently counselor, and pretty successful too, if I do say so myself. Closed on froggy days, the rest of the time the practice is heaving.

Here's the situation. Cold feet are a bit of a turn-off, but so are sweaty feet. I'd almost think, so saying, that I'd, if not solved, at least framed one of the existential questions.

Father deceased, but not before cursing me and cutting me off. With his cows he would talk about everything, only not about Franz and Franz's terrible sin. I was his pride, later his shame. A minister, then in the twinkling of an eye an incorrigible lecher, quite prepared to lose wife and child for it. That was too much, too much for the late Klemens Thalmann.

Somatically: Five eleven, skinny. Hair formerly chestnut, now a grizzle, face a puffy oval, glasses, of course, over spinach-green eyes. Ears small and pointy. Nose? Lumpy.

I feel sorry for anyone who wants to be anything he's not. It's respectable as an aspiration, but beware. I find myself groping for the thesis: The human soul is kitschy from beginning to end. You get your inner life off the peg. No mystery there, just schmaltz.

You know, they come to me with purple fingernails and sprouting Kaiser Bill mustaches, desperate attention seekers.

Then the minute they open their mouths, they spill out cliché. All the stuff they so deeply feel, desire, and dream is what in fact makes them so deeply unexceptional.

The one really arresting thing about you is your conk, the windings of your heart are strictly Tin Pan Alley. Proofs will follow.

What further facilitates my job: the identikit elements of what are termed "relationship problems." Truly delectable disharmonies I launch myself at with breathless excitement.

Yes, once in a blue moon!

But of course, our counselor, if he's not a simpleton, is under obligation to find the most banal situations "intriguing." If he scoffed at his customers' bellyaching, his practice would be empty.

I was a farmer's boy. No tree ever grew straight into heaven. Well-stuffed bellies, brains, souls were always foreign to me. Little is worthy of reverence. The pear falls and rots, but that's no reason to despise it. Man does more than shit, no doubt about it, but the thing is he shits as well, and generally with more enthusiasm than he ruminates; and yet we are told we are a creature of ratiocination.

People overestimate themselves and everything about them. Clearly, this platitude made me first a theologian, then an anti-theologian.

Conceived in sin like any son of Cain, and born in the bird-warble-warm February of the year 1935, a second son, to Klemens Thalmann and his wife Gret, née Habisreutinger. Given the rather humdrum baptismal name of Franz, and sent on my way with the motto: Man is like a breath. Psalm whatever.

Siblings. A brother, Paul, red-haired, kind, and wayward. Anna, favorite sister, died in '59 from leukemia. Myrta, married, criminally gentle mother of dorky kids.

Father, Klemens, deceased these past six months. Tumbled, or, if you prefer, slipped peacefully from off his milking stool.

His last will: Keep Franz away from my coffin.

Ten years of resentment for a rapscallion son. Of course, I went anyway. What could keep me away from the funeral held in elderflower-scented village cemetery.

Mother dead for as long as JFK. Dimming now, her freckles blend, I find, with those of my ex-wife Helen.

And now. Since when has Thalmann junior been haunted by his frog?

Since his father's passing.

Let me put it as simply as I can: The vengeful old so-and-so persecutes me from time to time by crawling into my throat. I have keen hearing, I can pick up the croak: "I may be dead, but you remain a twerp."

It is established that rectories are the best addresses. That's the way God wanted it. Mine was in the Zurich Unterland. A handsome half-timbered job, housing Franz with violin, Helen at the spinet, and ere long a little daughter, blond, Salome. Following the birth for the best part of the year more violin and spinet duets, then Costa Brava, and nine months later, a second daughter, Eva, also blond.

All in all, a prosperous time, much pleasure, unforced devotion, plenty of affection in spite of rubbers, the *spiritus rector* on the road, fizzing with evangelical zeal.

*

Do I drink? Not much. I wish I did. I drink as I live, without zest or regularity.

And I don't know anything. My own skin is a mystery to me. What is fire. I know they make wine from grapes, but what is a grape. The severe limitations on our understanding. Suddenly the refrigerator knows it must hum. Laughter comes easily, and the brain and the marrow are of the process as well, but what is the process. Yacking, hanging around, shaving, lots of stuff, and no one understands lettuce or electricity or cramp. "We must get the speed limit past its teething troubles." Whatever that means. I understand madmen, anyone who's been driven to religion, humility and evasions of every kind. I hate it all and indulge it.

Kindergarten and primary school in the village. Schoolmaster Knüsel: You should all take a leaf out of Franz's book.— I've always been a lazy so-and-so, and I don't regret it. My trick was to appear alert and engaged even when asleep.

Almost every man is bone idle. One must not say so. The industrious fellow, such is my understanding at least, is actually the particularly idle fellow, who from pure shame continually nips himself in the tail. As a child, galloping guilt complexes. Performance is only the screwed-up product of much idleness.

Secondary school in the next village along. The acne years. And dear God please do something about my clammy hands. Girls are unattainable, and for good reason. Confirmation classes by day, semenorrhea at night. Repression, anxieties, hang-ups, all that crap that retrospect likes to call youth.

*

No judgment is too sharp, no oath too coarse. The way puberty is handled in our latitudes is a scandal, chilling testimony to our brutal Christian idiocy. Generation hands down to generation the ruinous repression of wretched weekend fornicators, all the while pretending to be the lodestar of our civilization. In a word, the sinner needs God, and God needs the sinner, and so I duly found religion. With sports on the side.

A verse from Ecclesiastes, the son of David, King of Jerusalem. "Rejoice, O young man, in thy youth; and let thy heart cheer thee in the days of thy youth, and walk in the ways of thine heart, and in the sight of thine eyes."—What a message, dear brethren and sustren, but most particularly brethren. What do these words say to us, what do they osse? They say, in the language of our day: Chill. Dinna fash.—I continue in the words of Ecclesiastes, son of David, King of Jerusalem: "But know thou, that for all these things God will bring thee into judgment."

Grammar school. Yes, indeedy, little Thalmann gets into grammar school. He's taking Latin, would you believe. Schoolmaster Knüsel is propping up the bar in the Lamb and Flag, saying, oh yes, a bright lad, alert and industrious, I taught him his times tables and his alphabet, and, do you know something, his sister Anna is cleverer than he is.—What is it with those kids? asks Titus Feusi. Old Klemens hasn't got a gram more of gray matter than I do!—Yes, but unlike you, thus the landlady, old Klemens doesn't require seven glasses to get him in the mood, and so the product is bound to be different too.

In spite of myself, I'm falling into the schoolboy history essay manner. And then and then and then. Away with it. Pour me another and change of tack.

I'll tell you something, Froggy. From my practice. Case history, if you like.

The wife: I have to be super, or else he won't love me. The man: I have to be super, or else she won't love me. And both were borderline super, and lived in constant fear of being unmasked. And one day the wife said to the husband: I can't do it any longer, I'm not what you take me for, I'm not Grade A, and it's tearing me apart. And the man replied in kind. They went their separate ways—according to the formula— "so that each of us can find him/herself."

An everyday story, true and ever so slightly banal. It pays the bills. Scrub further details for now. Just this much. Mixed in with your sweet mother's milk is the ancient suspicion: Love must be earned. Any creature that just squawks and stinks deserves no adoring smile. Nothing's for free. Be other than what you are: Her blissful embrace will soothe the pain of pretense. (Hence the wish to be different becomes *de rigueur*. If you succeed with the transformation, then you will still sometimes feel the ape looking back at you from the mirror. And if you fail, you'll feel like a louse. Oppressive either way.)

How does a human react to a whispered: "I love you!"? With disbelief, of course. Surely shome mishtake, he thinks. I'm not the loveable kind.—But a couple then consists of two scaredy-cats lurching from one affirmation to the next, and the relationship ends when one party has had enough of the coo-koan and provocatively and proactively takes responsibility for his dandruff. (The entire process is called "finding myself" and—I say again—may be taken as a delayed response to a mother's bought smile.)

P.S. Clearly, a love that averts its eyes from our inadequacies will sooner or later lead us to squirm and belch out of orneriness, that finding-myself syndrome these days which I—as counselor and human—don't necessarily applaud.

I ventilate the room.

Since the divorce, I've taken up smoking again. I'd weaned myself off it when I got married. Not true, Helen made me kick the habit. Sweetie, she said, and more than once, your cigarettes stink and they're bad for you, won't you try not to, for my sake?—Whoa, I called, that's all I need, for your shitty lace curtains to outrank my three or four cancer sticks. And, anyway, your inveterate furniture polish stinks ten times worse. Of course, I said no such thing, in fact—back then—I didn't even think it. I of course, *for her sake*, refrained and also for her sake *laid off the vino*, and I preached to my confirmands: You don't need Dutch courage.

Try not to, for my sake!

Great Scott, and Franz lays off, and Franz is proud that Helen is proud of his strong will, and Franz never guesses at the secret kilotonnage of the little sentence: Try not to, for my sake!

*

In my office hours, I not infrequently see people, mainly women, marked by just such restraint and self-denial. Usually they have slim, wand-like figures, their eyes—blue, in the main—seem ever so slightly veiled, attractively bashful and just a tad brimming. They never have kissable lips, and they have a pronounced tendency to agree with me. Almost only women, as I say, married and with children. For years perfectly satisfied, then a sudden grinch. Weekly migraines, nausea, melancholy, the usual symptoms of self-denial.

"If any man will come after me, let him deny himself, and take up his cross, and follow me. For whosoever will save his life shall lose it: and whosoever will lose his life for my sake shall find it."

Only question is when.

There's a Bible verse with a bit of oomph. A recipe for leadership. Take a pinch of menace with a teaspoon of promises, and that's it, foolproof. There's a dish you can sink your teeth into. Helps you take the sting out of any rebellious and recalcitrant elements, anything that might say no to a hardboiled chef. Children, dachshunds, nations. The merely fearful is paralyzed. The merely hopeful jogs to excess. But the one who combines in himself hope and fear crawls.

A man comes into consultation hours and whispers: ED. Wife over breakfast let fall the fateful words: Albert could do it four times. Actuated by fear and by hope, he crawls under the sheets and at the same time stands over himself with his whip and thinks: Hup, Theodor!—Since then, something else has changed as well. Unasked, our Theodor vacuums the hall, buys flowers, guesses his Karin's every wish. But, he says, he doesn't feel good about any of it, he feels oppressed. I have the suspicion, he says, that in some corner of her soul, Karin is relishing my failure to perform, which she has caused.

Let's just let that stand for a moment, as a pert hypothesis.

Let us simply say that if a man were as free as propaganda would have him, then that would be the end. History, seen as marbled product of hope and fear, is finished if its subject is finished. Whereas this subject was, is, and will remain the crushed but ever-hopeful washout.

Back to our scriptural quotation. A shame. The way it differs so little from practical terrestrial wisdom. It sounds worldly to high heaven. A shame.

(The Savior of my dreams would say: Whoever wants to go with me, let him go. But I don't want anyone denying themselves or losing themselves. And don't let anyone think there's any virtue in picking up a cross. I don't care for Golgotha freaks. I'm not offering anything here, not even punishment. Let Adam and Eve eat whatever they feel like. No prohibition. And hence no sin. Be unbowed, make sure you get enough sleep and congenial silence, that's the most radical anti-devil medicine I know.)

Difficulties swallowing.

*

Strangely, our father never insisted that his sons be farmers. Maybe he was afraid of being pushed out to the cot. Never once did he say to me, when I was studying on my afternoons off: Why aren't you making yourself useful on the fields.—Quite the opposite, he would pat me awkwardly on the back: That's right, son, those potatoes aren't going anywhere.

Aside from that, he was strict and laconic. Grim. He punished the least failing. Not physically, or with words. Just by glowering.

He was a stranger to me.

The subsequent course of events makes me think I was still more of a stranger to him.

It's normal, though not actually laudable, for a person not to keep contact with his discharges. A chance fact which our philosophers disregard when they talk, as they sometimes do, about qualities that are specific to humans. And yet this is striking, and quite sets us apart from the other animals.

In brief, a little slime, joyfully/witlessly projected into a dark void, abruptly returns and lo! is become your son.

The wonder of it, the strangeness of it.

The standard thing is for the creator to be astonished by his creation, and the creation reciprocates, and astonishment is a mark of distance. One hears from artists of all sorts that they view a completed work, no sooner finished, as being in the nature of a stinky excrement. A part of themselves is therein contained, claims intimacy, and is yet rejected.

My father saw only this: His son, *the minister*, lets himself be wrapped around the finger of a sloe-eyed woman barely into her majority and villainously quits wife and holy office and children.

No, my father never really appreciated me, any more than I did him.

This needs to change.

If the frog won't recognize the spawn, then at least he should give himself to be recognized by it.

I grow lighter when I know what shadow hangs over me. And conversely, revenants find peace when they are understood.

2

KLÄR SAYS, You've been so grouchy of late, angry about everything, and you used to say: I'll never be such a crosspatch as Adam Sätteli as long as I live, he only sees the bad things in life. If I ever get to be like that, I want you to give me the bullet, that's what you said, says Klär, and now?

Sing hosanna with a catarrh. Let them be seventy-nine, and they won't be going tirra-lirra in their stalls, any bets. Young you sing, old you grouse, that's what old Adam said, and he knew.

Stand still while I'm milking you, damnit, you wretched nanny goat. Waser palmed you off on me, and I pay 4K for a bag of bones like that. A monument, Waser claims, a perfect specimen with exceptional performance. And what do I get? Four liters, four liters if that, and not a calf until January. And there's Waser thinking: I'll perk her up with some vitamin injections, and get some mug to take her off my hands.—And hey, there I am, simpleton to order, and I buy her, and no sooner is she under my roof than she smells bad out of one end and squitter-shits out the other.

It's like that with everything you buy, you're forever being duped, they do nothing but take advantage of you. Out of your savings you buy a sixty-hp tractor, and two days later it's standing trembling in a pool of oil. You buy a new toothbrush, and it sheds half its bristles the first time you use it.

Your clothes are either fraying or shrunk, your scythe is half rust, you don't own a can opener that works, you wipe your bum and the side of your hand's brown because that's the state of bog roll these days, for all the ickle flowers they print on it. They used to make products, now they make crap, so much for progress, and I don't care what Klär says. The more pitiful the wares, the prettier the wrappers they sell it in. Paul buys himself a ballpoint, Paul gets out of the institution and he wants to write letters to everyone, so he buys himself a new ballpoint pen, it's in heat-sealed plastic, Paul gets out the scissors, breaks the scissors, I kid you not, it takes Paul all of six minutes to extricate the pen from its shitty Fort Knox wrapping, and once it's out it's no good, and if it does write it writes for precisely two hours and not a minute longer, and then it's good for the bin, and that's how it is with everything, everything comes out of the factory bin-ready, buy anything and you buy crap, that's the truth by God.

Do you really have to wee when I milk your tits? Say, what kind of leaky vessel are you? Tell you what, I'll ship her straight back to Waser, let his machine suck on her again, there's nothing to be got by hand anyway, twisted little titties, all of it wrecked by the milking machine, just to save time, and for the sake of so-called hygiene, as though a couple of drops of cowpiss in the milk was a crime. Almost everyone these days has got something, and it used to be they were well by and large, that's where hygiene gets you, that's where progress gets you. Humans come into the world in hospitals and lie there in glass cases, Daddy smiles through the screen at the little sterile runt, and thinks: Can't believe I did that, what a dirty old so-and-so I am. Then it's the big day and the kid comes home, and you get the whole circus with germs and bacteria, and they spend the rest of their lives sickly.

Well, obviously. But then they just laugh at you. You don't dare say anything out loud anymore, no one takes you seriously. If you're over sixty, keep your trap shut, that's what they think nowadays. And if you give them a piece of your mind anyway, you'd be better off burping. And if you're past seventy, you're written off, a wizened old thing as far as they're concerned, a bag of bones that belongs in a shroud not a milking shed. You can do everything you ever did, milk, shovel dung, all the rest of it, they just shake their heads at you and pish: He thinks he's going to go on forever.—August Knüsel's been drawing a pension for sixteen years and he's about good for reading the paper. When he sees me, he says: Why don't you take a rest.—I can take a rest when I'm under the ground, I say. And they all urge me: Relax! Take it easy!!—And if you do, then it's: Old so-and-so's on his last legs.—And it's true, you just sit by the fire drooling, you feel worse every day, and sooner or later you shut up shop. 'S what happened with Ochsner, and Sutter, and Knüsel himself's a ham sandwich short of a picnic, see his head wobble around, you can tell he used to be a teacher, though in other ways he was right enough. We plowed the same furrow in our youth, Knüsel and me, and that was Dorli Zolgg. In May she was with Knüsel, in June with me, and in July Haas got to have a go. Then she qualified as a midwife, serving the locality, and now she's in the home, no more memory, just bubbles and squeaks, and that's how the time goes. Four times she delivered my Gret, did Dorli, and did it well. Helped me a lot later on as well, when dear Gret died on me twenty years ago, '63 it was, the twenty-third of November. There's me up at four, same as always, waiting down in the kitchen for her to come and bandage up my knee, and wondering what's keeping her. Gret! I yell, Gret! and I knock back my heart-starter, and when I go up to see what's what, she's on the floor, mumbling: I think I'm dying.—And I say, that's all I need, you'll be having one of your fainting fits, that's not going to kill you.—I lay her on the bed, she's gasping, I realize she means it, I call the doctor, it rings forever till his missus picks up and says she'll pass on the message. Then ten to six, Gret is dead, no doctor anywhere to be seen, twenty past he turns up, and says: Heart failure, most likely, my condolences, Herr Thalmann.—Four weeks later, the day before Christmas Eve, I get a bill, forty-one francs, would you believe it, son of a bitch, for a house call. What can you do. She's dead, in the cowshed the beasts are noising, a little after half past six I call Myrta my daughter, before I can open my mouth I hear her crying, I ask her: Do you know, then? She says I just heard it on the radio a moment ago, it's awful, and it's always the wrong people.—I'm confused: How can that be, it's not on the radio. She says: Why wouldn't it be, he was the president of the USA, after all.

That's how it is, and no one knows when it's their turn. Then Alexander Stoll comes up and he says: Klemens, he says, I'm not forcing you, but you can leave digging the grave to me, you've got enough on your plate.—I say, That's nice of you, Alex, but for now I'm still the gravedigger hereabouts, and duty is duty.—And I dug the grave for my Gret, the village was shaking its head, just like it is today, because I'm still working. I was fifty-nine then, Gret just fifty-three, and they all said: What's the betting next spring there'll be a wedding.—Well, they were badly mistaken. Klär my young-est sister moved in with me, freshly divorced from that Swabian layabout of a Stenzel, who did nothing but drink at her expense and mooch about, but that's what they seem to think is prime husband material. If you advise her against, that'll only confirm her in her choice, because she wants to prove she can save him. But Stenzel stayed in his swamp, there was no saving him, on the contrary, he dragged other women home with him and shagged around with them on the shag carpet at two in the morning, and Klär lying awake next door. That should have been enough for anyone, but no, she inherited her sunny good nature from her late mother. Experienced nothing but humiliation, Klär, nothing but disappointment, and still she sees only good everywhere, and if I ever get het up about anything, then she starts talking to me about old Sätteli, the grump.

Imagine the way he'd be running his mouth today if he could see everything going to the dogs, and the young people blundering about not knowing where bread comes from. Those conceited youngsters. They've got everything, everything, and they wreck it, they own cars and they ride the gears till the motor's wrecked and the tires explode, but that's the way they are with everything, everything's mishandled, mismanaged, misused, and anything and everything is done down and run down and still no one has the least idea where bread comes from. Take the way almost every phone booth is vandalized these days, you can read about it in the paper, the windows are smashed, the receiver's pulled out, the phonebooks are set alight, it's a disgrace, and it all takes its beginning in the nursery, where the little ones are stuffed full of everything from birth, they're spoiled and babied and petted and cooed over, they get given everything, there's nothing they haven't got or aren't allowed. You can give your grandson the Taj Mahal, do you suppose he'll even give it a second look. Or maybe just to pick it up and fling it across the room, and no one will spank his little bottom, and his mum says: Such a character.—And his dad, well, Daddy just reads the newspaper.

That's the way it is today, but it takes more than a fart to make a tempest, and one day things will change, no question, because what's built crooked is bound to fall. Maybe in a hundred years they'll all be saying: The young people back then, I've got two things to say about them, first they were given everything, and second it was all a drag.—That's the way it is, "it's a drag" is about the only thing you hear them say. Other than that they can hardly manage a grunt, they lounge around cheekily, even here in the country, and everything's a drag, except their tuneless music and their stupid bikes. They've got everything except proper parents, you need a magnifying glass to find parents these days, mostly they're hunting money, so they feel guilty, and they pump their kids full of money and crap, and you can read in the paper where that gets them.

Well, of course Klär's blind and refuses to see things are going to hell in a handcart. The young people are all right, she says. I see, I say, so two of these bikers almost hit an old man as he was crossing the road, and he wags his finger at them, and they see him and turn back and beat him to a pulp, and carry on on their merry way. That's today's world for you, I say, and if you ask me, it stinks, it's a vale of stink.—Just bad apples! says Klär, but I say: Harness up ten thousand oxen, then a plow the size of three cathedrals, and ho and hup and crack of whips, away with the lot of them, and when you're done, plant fresh.

Gret understood me. I was digging her grave like I was in a dream. Man proposes, God disposes, I was saying over and over, and the litany of my sins, first Anna, then Gret, not possible that she's put in this hole and is just gone forever, He coldly wrings her neck, I can't make sense of it, her icy skin, the terrible blank eyes, and it all used to be quick and warm, I stand there in the claypit, rest on my pickax, it's snowing, I'm full of hate, back home I grab the first cat I see and slam it against the wall.

Heart failure. Like Willi. He was a heating engineer and was returned to the Upper Chamber, and if he'd remained what he was, then they wouldn't have buried him yesterday. He'd have lived to be ancient, the size of him, keels over one day and amen, a tall gable, got too close to the lightning. And Titus Feusi goes and says: There was a shrewd Commie.—And I say: I don't care about that, he was a human being, maybe he was too clean for politics, he saw what was going on, and how the electorate is taken for a ride. They come up to you with their crooked grins and they say: Dear people, what do you think of this daylight savings time idea, shall we introduce daylight savings in this country, are you in favor, yea or nay?—And all the farmers say nay, and the people or a good majority of them say nay as well, and not long after that it's introduced, daylight savings, so I get up at three instead of four, the cows don't know if they're coming or going and they've no milk, and what kind of democracy is that? It would be more honest if they didn't ask us for our views. If a thing's really important, then they won't ask us anyway. If it's a bit of a detail, then they ask us and then do as they please, that's the way things are done nowadays, and I've had enough of it. I've been a patriot all my life, served more than a thousand days, more than done my duty, God knows, and been a law-abiding citizen. And all that doesn't matter a good goddamn, because one day the state comes up and kicks you in the behind and shoves a four-lane highway in your face, and you can yowl all you like, they'll stand there and wreck the country and destroy you. I've been a patriot all my life, and respected our leaders, They're doing a good job, is what I said, they're doing their best for the people, they're looking after our homeland, and I always said a simple soul like me can't compare with those lofty gentlemen. And then God knows what happened, it's out of whack, something feels wrong, for the last couple of years a different wind has been blowing, and other customs are in, and good sense is first taken advantage of and then roughed up and finally dumped. No one can lay an egg anymore, but the cackling is everywhere.

So now he's dead, buried, exited at sixty-five. I'm sure he saw and noted what was going off nowadays and that it's not him who's in charge, never mind the people, but the fattest wallets, and that's what broke him, you can say what you like. I've had enough of it now, politics, by and by you get their number, these lynxes sliming along the walls and grinning sweet and greasy, promising jobs and peace, freedom, fresh air, and the rest of it, we've heard that one quite a bit lately, fresh air is the big thing, and before the elections they play the national hero, we've heard it all, and it's a crying shame that people allow themselves to be diddled by any passing rogue. Twenty, thirty years ago, I remember saying all the filth from tailpipes and chimneystacks has to go somewhere, it doesn't just disappear, it has to go somewhere, is what I said, and so now they break it to us that it likes to settle on our lettuces. And that the trees can't cope with it anymore, well that's old hat as well, anyone can see everything is withered and drooping and going to rack and ruin, all sulphurated and syphilated, and those same fellows who five years ago giggled when someone was issuing warnings about the coming catastrophe and carrying on as per usual, those same titterers are now acting concerned and giving themselves airs, and promising emergency measures and accelerated programs, and suddenly the parties and the leaders and all the rest of them who live off lying and yacking, suddenly it seems they have a heart for the pines and the firs and the beeches and so forth, the mendacity of it is staggering, it won't go on a cowskin, and it's a monkey's shame, and every so often I think I understand my father and I think: I'm going to string myself up.

In the Lamb and Flag they say, Oh, it won't be so bad, you old misery, calm down, we have our freedom and if we were any farther east you'd have talked your way into prison by now, but here we're free and we determine what goes.— Who are you talking about? I ask, and Titus Feusi says: The people and you and me and everyone.—I say: Yes, you're almost right, if it's a question of footpaths and hiking trails, why then they allow us voters to mark our cross on a piece of paper, but if it's a question of billions for highways, that's something they need to decide by themselves.—Golly, says Oskar Mäder, this is some hand I've got. Klemens, isn't it you to lead?

I won't give her a name, that cow, not Selma, nor Lili, I'm giving her back. A noble beast, says Waser, a little high strung, but a splendid creature who'll make your fortune, he claims, she has a golden udder. What a blatherskite, golden udder, a shitty tail is what she has, and that's it, I want him to take her back, useless thing, a milch cow is what I need and not a pantomime horse, look at that, it's not even four liters, and that's with everything that's pissed out the back.

3

THE CULT of women and other persons of respect is put in handy perspective if one remembers: They too have digestive processes. This was a revelation of my younger years. My dear brother Paul, by contrast, found it a disabling insight that kept him from ever getting married, but more of that later.

Other than that, there's not much to say, I let Father be Father, the exorcism failed, my throat remains obstructed.

Kezi was her name, short for Kezia. She flooded me. Floored me. Bewitched and bewildered me. Kezi, you were my bit on the side, and at the same time the wave that washed me to safety.

"To safety"—eh? Ha ha.

Lay off yourself, Franz, keep to our agreement: No control, little control. No one is censoring you.

No one is censoring me.

That's easily said.

I know only one plausible definition of happiness: freedom from invigilation. Image of happiness: the hound Cerberus, dead as a dormouse.

Often, an image exists to show up the absence of what it stands for. As here. Happiness is remote. That's how it's meant to be. Bliss is scorned. We want walues, in other words: supervision. We seek fathers, rules and regulations. Give us the model that will crush us, the measuring rod that will show us what chipolatas we are.

Obedience. Belief. Suffering. Instructions followed. Expectations fulfilled. Said yes and please and thank you and three bags full, sir. Controlled stray impulses. Cleaned teeth, ditto ears. Swilled elderberry syrup. Studied the Good Book. Knew mastery and eventually self-mastery. Did what was dinned into me, and eventually started doing some dinning of my own. Shoveled snow. Madonnified women. Got in shape. Fiddled. Suffered. Was afraid. Could barely stand Father's glower. Rarely laughed. Prayed. Fed swine. Visited libraries. Mucked out the cowshed. Dogmas, apologias, ethics. Kissed Helen. Struggled for purity. Homiletics, catechesis, liturgy. Forswore eggs. Was afraid. Was good. Marriage. Ministry. And ever and over again, Amen. And always and in spite of all: persistent sadness and fear.

I say again, gladly: Happiness is remote. What's close is the head and within it the conscience that rampages harder the better behaved you are. Either/or: Self-scrutiny or happiness, choose one.

Cleared out the attic, threw all the rubbish away. My concern: The head empty of rubbish and without level crossing attendant will produce badness.—A rabid error. If I may say so: Dispense with tolls and your smuggling problem is over. Abolish the raised index finger, and some of the sources of evil will dry up. Castrate the fathers, gag the mothers. Delete your entry in the police records, fill for once your lungs.

*

I'm ventilating.

Kezi squeezed me. And I may say, wildly and with abandon.
I knew at once and for the first time: You stern Franz, now
you have no choice, the only possible way forward for you is
sin, and therefore it is no sin.

This was in the month of May. On a shrubbery lawn by
Lake Lugano. On a weekend retreat with Christian Youth.
Theme: Finding the Way to Thee.

At midnight with bladder full of Coca-Cola I absent
myself from the group, which is debating free will. Behind
a hazel bush, against my usual practice I answer the call,
while considering a way to refocus the fraying debate. Had
God not, I think to myself, left us the possibility of saying
yes or no with all our hearts (though guided, as ever, by His
Ten Commandments), then firstly He would not have pro-
mulgated said commandments, and secondly—without this
freedom—there would be no sin. We would therefore—again,
without our freedom—be as the beasts, pulled this way and
that by naked desire, which thank God is not the case, and
therefore we are free. What, I think to myself, is the matter
with this zip fastener. Is it jammed? It's jammed. I take a few
steps in the direction of the house, there's more light there,
and lean down and blow me: A piece of shirttail is sticking
out the front. Reverend, can I help? asks a voice of velvet.
There's just, I stammer in shock, there's just something got
caught here.—I'm an expert in these things, says Kezi, and
she takes me by the hand, and leads me down to a lakeside
bench. And no seamstress or mother could have solved the

zip fastener problem more deftly and less embarrassingly than Kezi. But her scent. Kezi enswathes me in a cloud of sweet jasmine for which I have no other word than divine. I suddenly have a yen to touch her. In the dark, her face is still more overwhelming than it is in the light, more haunting and gypsyish. I get a grip on myself and say: Well, better go, mustn't keep them waiting.—She gets up as well, and says: Oh, Franz, mustn't we.—And then it was that Kezi pressed herself against me, and I may say, wildly and with abandon.

To be continued.

A verse from Ecclesiastes, the son of David, the King of Jerusalem, has it: "A good name is better than precious ointment."

Almost every woman, my brother Paul is in the habit of saying, whiffs or stinks or leaks. I have, thus my brother Paul, no desire for a woman, just maybe one from the Orient, but not really.—Of course you do, I say, and it's so strong that it drives you to defame them.—You can speak German to me, says Paul. I say: Remember in Aesop, the fox cursing the grapes he can't reach, and saying they're probably sour anyway.—Old shrink claptrap! Paul growls, and bursts out crying and says: I've got red hair and bad breath and no one wants calloused hands.

Not a word against Helen. It wasn't her fault that, while strong, my love was not very sensual. And conversely: How is it a man's fault if (generally following the birth of a first child) his wife holds herself aloof and no longer feels entranced by his body? We have still less control of our sensuality than of other, supposedly nobler feelings. Those are bred, perhaps overbred, while the former is generally a browbeaten, hence unpredictable, mutt.

Kezi found him, breathed life into him. Shockingly inspirited, he leapt up from out of his tomb and began to dance. Anyone who has not felt this revival, be silent. He is equally remote from dog and man and God. And I instruct anyone: Whenas thy flesh yelpeth not, thy spirit is an arid waste.

Sensual awakening, admittedly, is often paid for in the currency of spiritual enfeeblement. That's as may be. What is enfeebled here is merely a deceptive carapace. Whatever is left of a person who avoids so-called sin is barely worth mentioning. But let me mention it anyway: a savorless gobbet of wretchedness.

Existential crisis. I've come to you, says a stammering customer, because I feel so strangely sad the whole time, because everything seems so meaningless to me.—(Correction: This was said not by one customer, but by very many; I select one at random, will call him Zemp, and here furnish an incomplete account.)

Growth: pycnic. Form: fleshy. Limbs: curt. Walk more a shuffle. Good blue eyes. Polyester easycare pants, hand-knitted cardigan. Our man Zemp is a primary-school master in his mid-forties, married with children, a major in the reserves.

Does your wife know about your condition?

No no.

You said no twice. Why?

I don't want to tell her, it would only burden her.

Can't she tell anyway?

I try and keep a lid on it.

So you have the feeling it would burden your wife if you told her how you really feel?

Yes, I do. I...I'm not so weak in other ways. I'm trying to fight it, and you, as an expert, I thought you would find the silver bullet.

What silver bullet?

The silver bullet against these moods of mine.

Are you not happy in your gloomy condition, then?

Not at all.

And the feeling that it's all meaningless, that seems inappropriate to you?

It's a virus. Just like a virus. An attack.

I will cut to the chase. Of course, the first part of my "treatment" is to show Zemp that even as husband and major and father he is allowed to show a little weakness; second, that problems of his kind cannot be treated by any "silver bullet"; and thirdly that his symptom is no more hostile than a lighthouse pointing out hidden reefs.—In the next phase, which I will call in the widest sense "political," it's a question of assessing whether feelings of gloom and futility cannot be understood as perfectly appropriate reactions (indicative of a yearning for intactness) to a reality, large stretches of which are so constituted that anyone not dispirited at its aspect ought rather to wonder at his failure so to react.

"Large stretches": Are there, I ask Zemp in a last phase, are there in your life any things or situations that you find unquestionably good and beautiful?—Zemp has a long think, and finally in a half-strangled voice he says: Tulips.

Anything else?

Zemp is silent for what feels like several minutes, and then he says: A proper French kiss.

And a little later, softly: A hot bath and the finale of Haydn's *Creation* and *filet de porc aux fines herbes*. Also the smell of violets.

And does all that have meaning for you?

Yes, but I don't ask myself that.

Provisional conclusion. The question as to the meaning of the French kiss is barely relevant. Lovely things are appreciated without meaning. Bliss is not met by a checklist. It would seem, therefore, that meaning—if at all—exists where it would be almost foolish to go looking for it. Sense, in Zemp's case—and we are all Zemps—is in sensuality.

Once it's been understood that our existential crisis is first and foremost a crisis of our senses, then in spite of metaphysical obfuscations we can see the therapy: The extension and promotion of sensuality. An expansion of the realm of the senses. Humanity will only have a future if we are successful in establishing a new Age of Tulips. The individual sets aside his gloom as soon as he feels his body is a house of joy. A precondition for this is moral enfeeblement, because morality has seen its role for thousands of years as an impediment to French kisses. To put it briefly: Traditional morality impedes sensuality.

Well. I'm not a philosopher, am I. I'm a put-upon frogman with too little oxygen.

*

Appendix 1: There will always be toothache. Also horseflies. Even in Paradise. That's OK. Without occasional gobbledy-gook, meaning would remain unapprehended, unheralded. (We are familiar with the downside of such long-established wisdom: On the one hand professional comforters, and on the other producers of pain, have long had recourse to it.)

Appendix 2: The first root of desensualization: The body is what blithely cacks its pants, the soul is what feels bad about it.—The second root: Only the distant, impalpable God is without stain, and idols are a mean lot.—Third root: Even pleasure palls. So much for illusion.

Appendix 3: Zemp is doing much better.

To return to the night in May. Suspicion is not rife in these circles. One puts one's hand in the fire for Pastor Thalmann. And if he had been gone an hour with Kezi (and not just ten minutes), he would have been "getting some fresh air" and giving some sound advice to Kezi, because her faith is infirm, and she was once—according to her welfare author-ity—described as neglected.

In a word, we rejoin the group, concealing our *après*-state of fluster, and take up the struggle where we left off: Is hu-man destiny foreordained by the Divine Will? Does His absolute power not rule out the self-will and freedom of His creation? How can a mover and shaker move and shake if the world is full of autonomous beings, forever spoiling His plan!—What about a little fruit salad? inquires a velvet voice, and all are delighted and go *Yum!* as one.

*

For ten weeks that summer, Kezi was something like a secret wife to me.

And not just me. No details. Just the coarse facts: From the middle of July, passing water started to become a fiendish torment to me. Reverend, says the GP, I'm afraid you have the clap.—I what? Good God, how could such a thing happen?—Reverend, let me be frank: Your relationship with a certain half-gypsy girl, pardon my saying so, is almost as much common knowledge as said gypsy girl's, pardon my saying so, casual lifestyle. I will assume the only person in the entire village not to know about it is your wife, and as your medical confidant, I suggest you do something about that as soon as possible.

That same day the president of the local church told me it was impossible for him to turn a blind eye any longer, he had, on behalf of the congregation, to advise me to step down. And did you know Kezi Moser is the subject of a court case?—A court case? Because of me?—I would hope not, Reverend, rather because of all the others.

Sentence is passed in late autumn. The act as such is termed public indecency, but, even where money changes hands, there is usually no legal sanction for it. What was decisive in this instance was where it took place. It transpired—whatever you like to call it—in a cemetery in the local town. Kezi's behavior qualified as persistently disturbing the peace of the dead.

Have another, Franz, why don't you?

*

I myself never met Kezi in that cemetery. As a venue, it would have failed to charm. It's not right to strive for an excess of romanticism. Admittedly, I wasn't appalled when I heard the details from our otherwise necrophiliac press, this time all aquiver with indignation. In fact, if there was anything disrespectful and macabre, then it was the stir they created.

Try visiting the city of Fez in Morocco, and seek out the vast and wonderful cemetery there. It is, I contend, a place of life. Snow-white graves afford privacy and shade to lovers, and excited children go skipping and yelling over their ancestors. People picnic there and void, and under a stunted almond tree a couple of barbers shave their customers. The dead participate in life, and the living are close to their dead. All as it should be.

The idea that our dear ones would take umbrage at life going on over their heads seems highly improbable to me. The peace of death is an invention of those who are on the warpath with the reaper: A noisy sign of life might provoke him. The tiptoed hush in our cemeteries may pose as respect but is in fact an expression of blind panic. Ideally, they would see all death barred, graveyards as a no-go zone, admission only for corpses.

So no, I didn't share in the general indignation. I was merely sad, endlessly sad.

For Helen, it meant divorce. The Bible, which one read every day, exhorted forgiveness. Life followed other laws. I kept begging her to forgive me, God knows, and I insisted on the absolute truth: Helen, I like you, I want to stay with you.—The memory of her high, mocking laugh makes me shudder to this day. Go and lie with your harlot, you filthy liar, don't touch me, keep your hands off the children, go away, begone.—And Helen's father, a distinguished professor in water management and president of the Evangelical Synod, told me down the telephone: A fellow like you deserves a sound whipping followed by prison.—My own father meanwhile came to see me in his Sunday suit, looked me up and down trembling, dully said one word, and left. "Disgrace." That was his last word to me. I never saw him again.

A good deed is easily accounted for: There's nothing complex about decency. What's mysterious is the fall from grace, while the sinner is positively unfathomable. No protocol captures him, no witness and no judge ever guesses at the truth. Here is the trespass, the motive dividing and subdividing hundredfold, and there the limited number of preformulated sentences, of clumsy expressions of indignation and explication. Everything so inchoate, so endlessly inadequate and overblown.

For instance, how many people know that a zip fastener occasioned my fall, and that, without it, I would still be a minister of the church and husband to Helen? I alone. And then even that hindsight is only provisionally acceptable, a prop and a soft crutch. Back then on Lake Lugano, I could have said to Kezi: It's nothing, my shirttail's got stuck, I'll fix it, you go back inside, I'll be along in a jiffy.—I didn't say those words. Why not? Because what followed was bound to follow, because—for reasons that would have seemed obscure to me then—I was ripe and receptive for a turn.

The true reasons have since been (at least partially) reconstructed, perhaps even constructed, because no one working backwards can get by without speculation. Historians are poets *manqué*, sniffers who follow any tracks without ever getting the bunny. I say two things, as everyone will. Firstly, it had to happen, and secondly (in hindsight) I'm glad it did.

As for "the true reasons": The weakest link in any chapter of accidents is soon found. Three weeks before, Helen—for a short break—was in Merlischachen on Lake Lucerne with her friend Elsa Wolf. And sent me a postcard from Merlischachen!—Now excuse me, is that any way for a spouse to behave?! Does wifey communicate with hubby by postcard? Is not a postcard the sign par excellence of superficial friendship, and hence of chilling distance? All right, agreed, maybe not so bad, only what Helen wrote on it, that gave me pause. She wrote (you see, I can't get it out of my head): Hey Schnäggli, I'm sending you love and kisses from Merlischachen, the lake looks very crowded with all the sailboats, see you soon, H.

Perhaps you find that adorable. But I felt comprehensively alienated, and for several minutes our years of intimacy were extinguished. I kept reading the card over and over again. I see, so the lake looks very crowded with all the sailboats, does it indeed, well, isn't that nice. And suddenly in my head there bulked this monstrous sentence: I'm so bored with Helen's bony legs and boring behind.

This postcard, as already said, is a weak link. But the quest for causation must not despise weak links; apparently negligible factors add up and—especially in a marriage—become weighty. (As a counselor one often notices them—the negligible factors—acquiring the force of gale warnings. For many couples this is the moment they are moved to take professional advice in the first place.)

But there's an end of the Merlischacher matter. It contributed, as indicated, pretty minimally to the calamity that followed. There are graver matters to be adduced. Whereof more later.

I empty both ashtrays.

Frog here or there. In spite of all, persistence of positive, almost tender feelings. No hatred, only a sort of counter-grouse from time to time. Also impatience: Father, abandon me. No need to kill the fatted calf for your disgraceful son, just let him breathe a little easier. Why so unforgiving. You were hardly without stain yourself. You were human as well.

4

TAKE FOR example calving. The way it used to be, and the way it is now. You used to walk into the cowshed in the morning, and there was the new calf, up on all fours, frisky and ready to go. Everything went like clockwork, plup, and it was out. And now? Well, it seems the animals are no longer up for it, God knows why, almost every other cow is a tight fit and needs the vet, and the calves are lying transverse, and they want to be pulled out by the heels, arsey-versey, and if you want my opinion, first, the beasts are overbred, and second, there's a murrain on artificial insemination, but what can you do, it's what there is nowadays. There aren't any proper bulls anymore, maybe the odd one in those breeding institutes in Zurich or Bern, and they have it tapped out of them, but we don't really like that, do we, eh, Rösli? You never made a fuss, I'll say that for you, come on, get up, it's only lately you calved again, fifth time now, three weeks ago. You give them barley meal in the last five weeks till they calve, that's what my late father used to do as well, barley meal and oats, that's the old recipe, isn't that right, Rösli, and then grass and hay at the finish. What do you suppose old Waser would give you? Straw and arugula and cornflowers, but that's because he's not a farmer, he's an amateur, his hands are about right for eating yogurt. A fine beast, long-suffering and well behaved, the udder powerful, and with a spray you could extinguish a house fire with, eleven liters morning and night, yup, they can't believe it at the co-op. He can't milk anymore with those ancient hands anyway, that's what they think, and they grind their teeth when they empty your full can each time, yup, it's Thalmann on the job.

Sixty-one years ago, in the French part, when I was a little farmhand learning the ropes, back then they still had bulls, by gum, no artificial insemination then, and oxen for tractors. And there was one cow in the cowshed, queer, I hated her on sight and she me, and one day she gets bucky, and each time I clean the cowshed she lashes out and kicks and barges like there's something the matter. In every other respect, a super milker. One Sunday evening, there I am spreading straw, and again she lashes out, and I think, that does it, and I hold out the hayfork a little, and promptly she kicks into one of the tines with her rear hoof, and the next day she has a beautiful swelling on her hind leg, and the farmer's hopping up and down, the vet comes and treats her, and none of it does any good, she's off her feed, she loses weight by the day, she can't stand or walk, she has to be put down, says the vet. Apprentice! calls the boss. Put the oxen to, and take the cripple cow to the renderer.—We drag her out, four of us, it takes us half an hour to get her lying there in the cart, and then I drive off. I stop outside the renderer's, climb down off the cart, go inside and say straight out: *Voilà la vache.—Bon*, says the man, spits in his butcher's hands, let's be having her then.—And as we step outside, there's nothing there, no cart, no oxen, no nothing, just a cloud of dust on the horizon, we set off running, the butcher and I, and we find a pile of rubble at the edge of the village, the cow's lying there in the middle of the road, the cart smashed against a poplar, and the two oxen grazing outside the cemetery wall. You'd better clear off, you little shit, says the butcher, you'd only get in the way.—I shog off with the oxen, and as I'm turning into the farm, there's the farmer just emerging from the cowshed, and he asks me what I've done with the cart.—I say: *Foutu.*—And he yells back: Foo what? and sits down on the dungheap, and looks at me long and hard, and then he says: Thalmann, you're the devil.

Two weeks later there's the thing with the farmer's wife, what a fool I was, I'm standing on the little wooden balcony outside my room, it's a clear night, and I'm thinking: Everyone's asleep.—And suddenly the farmer's wife pops up next to me, she's almost thirty, I'm eighteen, and a shooting star crawls down the sky. I made a wish, she says, and I say: What? and she whispers: Everything! and she lays her head on my shoulder, and whispers: Come on.—*Ça ne va pas*, comes my strangulated reply, *le patron, le patron.*—She says: *Le patron dort toujours*, and in German she says: Come along, you chaste Joseph.—And suddenly I think to myself: I only get to be young once.—But then you don't need a run-up to step in a cowpat. No sooner is my little light out than I hear a wheezing up the chicken ladder, the door flies open, and the farmer's in the room. He sets his lantern on the chair, he's strangely quiet, motions to his wife and hisses: *Va-t'en!*—She scurries off, and there we have it out, Jesus, I didn't even try and defend myself, and the next day I'm sitting on the train home. And Uncle Max, who has run the farm since my father's death in 1916, shakes his head at me, and says: What's going to become of you? Six years later, in 1928, I take over the farm, and since then fifty-five years have passed.

You can't say I don't understand young people, I was young myself once, and in time we'll all be angels in heaven, I say to Klär, but that doesn't mean we'll ever behave like the young people today. There was such a thing as respect once, and today they walk past you, the young people, and they look you in the eye without shame, and they don't open their mouths to greet you, and what do you think their parents have to say about it? You can't expect manners, they say. When earlier it used to be: Now say, Good morning, today it's: You can't force them to do something they don't want to do. And you can see in the paper what that leads to. If you don't prop a tree, the growth is slow and crooked, and that's the way it is with children, at least that's how I see it. Open a newspaper and you won't believe your eyes, nothing but sports and indecency and murder, there are break-ins all over the place, property being stolen and made away with. They never catch the culprits, ever, and if they happen to nab one, then it's always: Oh, a bad childhood, oh, a rough adolescence, oh, poor devil.

Ernst Stettler lives in a house on the edge of town, he and Ida his wife, and they both ride bicycles. One Tuesday morning, Ernst's bike is missing, it was parked in front of the house and it's not there, he goes to the police to report it. On Wednesday there's a knock on the door, and it's a young man with the missing bicycle, and he says: Yes, I took it, but my conscience, my conscience wouldn't leave me alone.— Apologizes over and over again, and says he'd like to give them a little something to make up for their trouble and inconvenience, and pulls a couple of theater tickets out of his pocket, for Friday night. Ida is all moved, and so is Ernst, and in bed that night Ida says: You see, good things happen still, only they don't get written up in the paper.—Ernst says: Well, I could write a letter about it, and Ida says: Yes, why don't you.—On Friday they go to the theater. Coming home at the end of the evening, they see the front door's been broken open, half the house is emptied out, rugs, silver, clock, her jewelry, everything gone, and in the bathtub they find a waterlogged note: Hope you had a good time at the theater.—That's how things are done nowadays, and they never catch the villains, and if they do, then as I say it's, oh, bad childhood and all the rest of it. My father hangs himself in 1916. In 1920 my mother falls off a ladder, on October eleventh, picking pears, and she picks herself up and laughs and says: I'm made of india rubber.—She touches her head and falls down in a faint, five minutes later she's dead of an aneurysm, and did it set me on a path of crime? No one in the world knows how I suffered, I'm the last person who would shout it from the rooftops, and today you can commit burglary, assault, murder, and you'll always be excused, you'll always find extenuating circumstances, in the end you'll always be found to be of unsound mind, no one who does evil these days is to blame, no one needs to suffer the consequences of their actions, because all he is is a poor victim himself, and in the end the Big One will come along, and everything will be wiped out, and it won't have been anyone's fault.

My father came home on furlough in February 1916, I was twelve, he was sitting at the kitchen table, shivering, and said: People are evil. We're climbing from Flums-Grossberg up to Madils meadow, I'm carrying my rifle and pack, and our lieutenant gives me a box of ammo to carry as well, another sixty pounds, and Private Kobler says to me: Tell you what, you carry the box until we get to the meadow, and then I'll take over until the Broder Alp, that's nothing but my duty as a Christian.—It's twelve below centigrade, and by the time we're on the Madils I'm soaked through and knackered and I drop the box into the snow and tell Kobler: There you go, Herbert, all yours, thanks a lot.—And Kobler says: I wasn't born yesterday, you carry it yourself.—I say: But, Herbert, that's what we agreed.—He says: Oh, kiss my ass.—I say: You're a rotten bastard.—And he says: Aw, shall I get your mummy to dry your tears, then, you little baby, you wretch, you weakling.—I hit him in the face once or twice, not hard, and the lieutenant comes tramping up and yells: Thalmann, I'm disappointed in you, that'll cost you your next furlough, we're moving on, I want you to carry the box now, and that's an order!

My father told us the story haltingly, at the kitchen table, and he was pale and shaking, and my mother laid her hand over his, and said: But there are so many good people as well.—And he got up right away, and said: Wickedness rules, I'm going to see to the cowshed now, I want no help, Gustav, and you, Klemens and Wendel, you're to shovel snow, you can hardly get out the front door.—And with that, Father went to the cowshed, and that's where shortly after seven Wendel found him.

Suddenly everything's at an end, the minister's speaking about our home in the sky, and they put you in the ground, and then everything goes on, and no sooner has your gravestone put on moss than it's taken down, there's no space, no sooner have you rotted away than you hear the pickax and shovel, they're putting in the next one, and your teeth have got company, and your rotted ribs go on crumbling away together with a fresh set, and so it goes. I've buried the dead from three communes for almost thirty years now, on average that's five per annum, and each time I thought: One day I'll understand what I'm doing, one day I'll even understand death, and I've buried friend and foe, I've buried my Gret and my youngest daughter Anna, and I always thought: One day it will dawn on me, one day I'll understand the mysteries, one day while I'm digging a voice will pipe up and tell me what it's all about, and why and what for and whither bound. Nothing, nothing's happened in all those tens of years, and now I'm old, and I'm milking Rösli, and I don't understand either God or his creation.

Perhaps I should have read more books, maybe that's where I would have learned what matters, I don't know, I'm a little doubtful. I probably haven't read more than a dozen in my life, when did I have time for reading, there was never a moment. Anna read a lot, especially on her sickbed, and she often said: Daddy, listen to this, and she'd read me something, and it was always something sad. What are these things that you're reading, I would say, they're not right for you. And Anna said: If you're going to die, you're allowed to be sad.—Anna, I said, you're not dying, you'll fight the illness, I'm certain, and Anna smiled and three times read something to me, no, it was four or five times, and her face is pale and teary, and I stand there helplessly, and I won't forget the words as long as I live, "hearkens the ear to the gentle plaint of the blackbird in the hazel bush."*

I think the fellow that wrote that wasn't a happy bunny either, those fellows rarely are, that's why most of them die young, as do the scholars. If you own a dog, I read in the paper, you live longer than if you don't, maybe that's true, maybe it's not, I have no idea, you read all kinds of things in the paper. Either way, everyone's number is up eventually, in olden days the plague got you, today you're run over, used to be you starved, today you'll more likely die of overweight, our little nation is lugging twenty-five thousand tons of excess weight around, it says in the paper, madness, you let

*From Georg Trakl's poem "Stunde des Grams" ("Hour of Grief").—*Translator's note.*

the others shrivel while your own rump thickens. You need to keep your strength up, people say in these parts, and they stroke their paunches and eat themselves to death, Lord knows, the country isn't what it used to be, you see the signs everywhere, and when Klär gets the flag out of the chest of drawers to put in the window for the First, my heart doesn't beat the way it once did, which I think is a pity. Wealth makes you fat and cosseted and disagreeable, and I wouldn't be rich if you paid me to, even if you're allowed to do anything you like if you're rich. There are masses of millionaires among us, and everyone does just exactly as he pleases, and pilfers money through hundreds of nooks and crannies, and is looked up to as an upstanding citizen, and if he's out of luck he's caught with his fingers in the till, and he happily pays his pittance of a fine and goes back to being a fine upstanding citizen again. But if you're a farmer or a dairyman that's been known to skim the milk or water it down, then you get put in chokey, and you're finished, that's the way it goes. All citizens are equal before the law, it says in the constitution, quite so, I say, it's only the scales of justice that are unequal. Hans breaks a window; Fritz breaks a woman's eye. Hans gets put away, and Fritz is acquitted, and Fritz is a policeman. Hans pinches a fifteen-year-old in the bottom, Fritz kicks a twenty-year-old in the belly. Hans gets put in jail. And Fritz is acquitted, because Fritz is a policeman. And then you sit around in the Lamb and Flag with your pals from the shooting club, and you tell them what you think about it, and they get all het up and say: You Commie swine, since when have you been a friend to hooligans and streetwalkers?—I say: Don't talk rot, we need the Law, I can see that, and I don't like demonstrators any more than you do, but an injustice remains an injustice, and what's skewed is skewed, you've got to see that.

I don't go to the pub so much anymore, I've got Klär here, and I've got the cowshed, and every so often I can understand the young people. So many old people don't want to know, and they're so blind and set in their ways, and they always talk the same rot, so sometimes I tell myself: You know what, you're moldering away yourself. That's why I enjoy milking, when you're milking you can think, you can argue the whys and wherefores of this and that, and that way you stay alive in your mind a little, isn't that right, Rösli? Eleven liters in fifteen minutes, you're a doll.

5

AND WHAT if the farmer had been fast asleep that starry night? Eh? What then, you rapscallion? Then the little pren-tice would have quickly helped himself and with flushed cheeks and racing pulse slithered into a life of sin.

Never mind.

I know, my case was different, I know, you old tormentor.

Franz is a chip off the old block, Franz is as tough as you are, as tough as your fist clenched in his throat. The night is long, I've got time.

He had what people used to have: principles. And if it hadn't been for our mother, who would occasionally knock an airhole through the hermetically sealed borders of our up-bringing, then we would all have suffocated.

I can remember almost nothing of my childhood. I see myself as a stiff little boy who spilled his milk and sought through tears to preempt his father's glower. Hopeless! He was implacable. And hence punished both transgressions: the clumsiness and the tears. And of course he meant well.

Wherever I ran to and however quickly, a fatherly prin-ciple was there waiting for me: I knew you'd come.

So what did I do? Two things. I became, from the outside, a model pupil, and in my secret heart of hearts a recalcitrant so-and-so. And then I bonded deeply and trustingly with the Almighty. But He saw everything, including also my disobedient core. I had inadvertently recruited a second master.

"Finish your porridge!"—Yes, father, I said, and thought: No, you brute.—And I finished my porridge, and in bed begged God to forgive me my wickedness.

Early on, Franz felt: Authority has two faces, one kindly, one menacing. Whoever can protect me can also punish me. The shepherd's crook promises security, but God help the lamb bleating out of turn.

Protection is also supervision. Feelings of security and fear are so direly twinned that we trustingly approach on all fours those powers that intimidate us, thinking they will shield us and protect us. People are always beating a path to power. Might can crush its fans, cut a swathe through its disciples, and yet remain a place of pilgrimage. God torments Job, Job remains His servant. God delivers His one son to the knife, and he remains His son. I know women who are helplessly smitten—yea, smitten—with the forearms of their husbands who daily beat them.

Reuz was his name, steely voice, stern jaw, and thin lips. High-school teacher. Tyrant. Man without mercy. We quaked before every class. What mood will he be in today? Will he slaughter us? There is a deathly silence when he enters, and all spring instantly to their feet because anyone a second late will catch it. I avoid Reuz's eye. Eye contact increases the chances of being called upon. And besides, his expression is unendurably dour and gives no hint of what will come. Good morning, class, he says patriarchally, today we are doing... nothing.—He smiles impishly and says: We're going to take it easy today, if that's all right with you.—And we smile back, not even strainedly, but with real calm, the shaking is over, the terror gone, old Reuz, what a mensch, he has followers, more than his milder colleagues, Reuz is popular.

Father makes an exception. The teacher looks the other way. The colonel allows the men to go on home leave earlier than he might have done. The president issues a pardon. The Almighty doesn't take things as far as He might, and if He does torment you, He blesses you afterwards and gives you a thousand she-asses and fourteen thousand sheep and oxen and camels and a long life.

Authority looks humane every so often, then the populace believes it is better than its reputation. It always makes a good impression, for instance, when a pol plays with his little pooch. The occasional appearance in shirtsleeves can work wonders. And if the potentate appears in bathing trunks, then his subordinates heave a deep sigh of relief, redouble their loyalty, and paddle along beside him with a merry tune in their hearts.

We know all that. Almost everyone meekly obliges, sees his life's goal as being a serviceable spear-carrier in an absurd drama, almost everyone takes his studied feeble-mindedness for cleverness. Stupidity is trumps, wall-to-wall prating, mingled with incorrigible obedience. Skeletons are at the tiller, and exhort their fat followers to treachery. The corrupted Babbitt who strips down his wife and motor on Saturday and watches the big game on Sunday rules. The ideal is the twisted soul, because that alone is considered normal and digestible. Soberly, i.e. in the light of bygone reason, there is nothing more gruesome than a brood that prides itself on its simplemindedness and venality. Here the borderline infernal is put into practice, here the most wretched acts are perpetrated, here nothing but nothing exalts us.

Back a few. Contemplate distance strategies. I don't trust the ironist. His contradiction has too much diction. He solicits agreement, which makes him social and vain. A lonelier soul is the self-ironist, at home somewhere between masturbation and masochism. He gives evil a green light, because he doesn't take his own sufferings seriously. To smile at oneself is stage suicide. The self-ironist seeks a double detachment: He withdraws from the world and pokes fun at himself, dreaming in feeble hours of an opposite number that won't find him contemptible. And cynics? I don't care for them. They stand on one leg in a swamp whose existence they deny. They are participants. They do the wrong thing in full knowledge that it is wrong, and that is their form of distance from error. To the cynic, nothing is sacred, not even his own despair. Not that—self-ironically—he smiles at it: He denies it. One might as well have the north wind as despair that denies itself.

Humor, though. Almost eludes description. Strangely adorable bastard child of love and wistfulness. Humor doesn't rant and won't curtsey. Perfectly unassertive, tentative, sheepish, it proposes conciliation. Humor is warm and dark green, in the midst of futility it blooms. Bravely and enigmatically.

(As a onetime theologian, I must admit: There is not much evidence of this growth in the Book of Books. The prophets and apostles are too embroiled in their business. They give vice the rough edge of their tongues, but bliss too is a serious matter and requires a high tone. The Messiah is occasionally sarcastic, but there's never a belly laugh in him. God the Father, though! In my rare moments of boisterousness, I like to think of Him as a humorist, because He has everything you need for the role: distance and love, a sympathy with frailty, and quite a lot of justifiable melancholia.)

Little Priest. Do we have to have a sermon tonight then? Do you imagine your strenuous croon would chase off a frog?

Leave me be. I believe what I believe, I do what I do, I ask for the kindness of no questions, please. I would like to silence the voice continually chiding me. I would like to fall silent myself, perhaps silt over altogether on some quiet beach.

But it's too early for that still. I turn fifty next year. Sometimes I feel so sluggish it's as though I had black blood in my veins. Then I gulp vitamins and—lately—ginseng, and after getting up I touch my toes twenty times, and do a rubbery grimace in the mirror. You have to fight back. The profession insists on it too. A run-down counselor isn't much of a draw.

No, there's no hurry about the silting-over. Perhaps I'll even achieve union with myself and the world first. There are some positive indications. In bright, hyperalert moments, I have a sense: Everything is worth loving, even Franz. Then again, I have other moments, equally sharp and equally sensitive. And in these other moments, I have the sense: Everything is worth hating, especially Franz.

*

If you synthesize the two extremes, you come to—in my case—this result: I am not saying the world should be condemned with all its works. There are some nice things in it. To lay stress on these is the done thing nowadays, I know; I say it anyway, I say it in contradiction to those runaways who poke fun at their yesterday's disgust and who today present themselves in fashionably positive colors. My fundamental dislike remains, my weltschmerz is unaffected, though I remain a devotee of lush grass and cloudless skies. Women, too, if I might make so bold. So long as they have gentle eyes and eschew chitchat. And they leave seducer types in soft shoes and shades standing or sitting. So long as they are not kitteny or eyelinerish, don't take out that oven-ready chicken dish which they assume—and unfortunately usually correctly—reliably charms the masculine world. Her voice is a woman's most doubtful organ, and if it checks out, one must be duly grateful. (O Kezi.) After that the nose, very problematic, often an Achilles' heel, even when condemned to support a pair of spectacles. (O Helen.)

So I'm multiply in love. From time to time I'm lenient with myself, though rowdy self-approval was never my thing. I must be content if a measure of sympathy emerges. It's the best I can do. A seminar in Boston only briefly shook at the roots of that, a seminar in which I was instructed to find myself OK all down the line starting before breakfast. Since all the other participants also assumed I was hip, and since even the seminar leader didn't turn me away on a no-moon night, I returned to Switzerland in a state of some elevation. A customs inspector in Zurich gave me a cool reception and asked me to open my suitcase. I started to shake. I had a pressed cake of hash wrapped in tinfoil in my sponge bag. The inspector failed to spot it. He finally gestured impatiently and muttered: OK.

At night I lay awake a long time and found the episode speaking and full of lessons.

I'm reminded of Herr Mumpf. He too was a customs inspector. To him I owe an insight into our sometimes eccentric spiritual conformation. Mumpf was a real man and then again not. Mumpf is a fictive but thickset customs inspector. Dense coal-black mustaches.

Frau Oberholzer came to counseling for chronic constipation and onychophagy. Another term might be "biting her fingernails." Anyone scratching or nibbling or rubbing away at themselves is punishing themselves for something or other. The chewing itself is frowned upon, and calls for a further round of punishment. This is where constipation comes in: You punish yourself by not properly digesting this thing that you so reprehensibly eat. Such was—greatly simplified, of course—my approach to the case. Frau Oberholzer was in her fifth year of marriage. In our fourth session she said: My husband hardly ever kisses me, and when he does it's never deep kissing.—Hm, I reply. On the other hand, says Frau Oberholzer, he takes me every night.—I see, I say, that sounds like good news, provided you enjoy it yourself.—Oh, it's quite wonderful, says Frau Oberholzer wistfully, and she has a little cry. A few minutes later, there's a halting admission: And I deceive him shamelessly, every night.—Are you telling me you have congress every night with *two* men?—Yes and no, she says lingeringly, as though hoping I would come upon the solution myself. But my brow stays furrowed, until finally

Frau Oberholzer says, with a measure of irk: I just happen to need a customs official, without Mumpf I would never be able to climax.—So Mumpf is his name, I mutter, since I can't think of anything more sensible to say. Yes, she says eagerly, I call him Herr Mumpf and use the polite *Sie* form, he is a very strict customs official who always keeps his uniform on, the best is when he catches me red-handed, that drives him wild, but you must know that Mumpf isn't really there.—Aha, I say, so you just imagine Herr Mumpf, he is a fantasy figure.—Unfortunately, she says. My husband is a baker, but I forget that as soon as he turns the light off. Nights when I don't forget it, in other words, when I tell myself, Oh, it's not Herr Mumpf at all, it's Ferdinand, all my satisfaction vanishes just like that, I've tried it often enough.—I see, I say, and this whole business is a weight on your conscience?—That's the thing, she says, that's why I need Herr Mumpf to come and punish me all the time.

I'll break off here. I frankly admit this degree of deviousness was too much for me, though generally I welcome complexity. I passed Frau Oberholzer on to an analyst who told me six months later that he had made some progress and that she was now on first-name terms with her Herr Mumpf.

It's a widely known phenomenon that within a marriage sexual fantasy runs riot. The thing one so passionately desired is now a constant, bulky, possibly snoring presence. The new state of constant mutual availability is beguiling for a while, but the shriveled desire and balked fantasy then recover and spread far beyond the thing that once satisfied them and now sits yawning on the sofa. The intramarital solution to the problem consists in revising the familiar bedmate, turning him or her into someone else for the minutes in question, who, while he or she may have the identical style of panting, appears nevertheless spicier. The fact that this minor metamorphosis saves many couples from adultery is actually a blessing, if you think about it, and yet it is subject to far harsher taboos than actual adultery.

I can well imagine that the baker Oberholzer has fantasies of his own, and enjoys imagining for a few moments that it is Frau Zeberli, the owner of the next-door tearoom and his best customer, who is sighing under his ministrations. And that in turn would give rise to the wholly ethereal Mumpf-Zeberli couple, so that probably one would be right in saying that there inheres in every couple a capacity for adaptation that makes a marriage something of a *Märchen*. Or a menagerie.

When you drink this magic potion, every woman will be a Helen.—Absolutely: What Doctor Faustus is swilling is the power of imagination, the poetical gift of revising women into beings that suit his desire. But meanwhile, who was it brewed the drink, who handed Faustus the cup? A witch. And on the say-so of boss Satan. *Voilà.* The imagination is devil's work, as Frau Oberholzer well knew. Hence her guilty nail-biting.—Nonsense. The case is more complicated. In her mind, Frau Oberholzer is making love with an organ of the state; and then—to mollify her conscience—she declares the same organ with which she has been making love to be a penal organ, to punish her excess. (That's how endlessly resourceful the soul of woman is, perhaps even the soul of man as well.) Now, how do we interpret the nail-biting? As further punishment, for her devious psycho-logic? As a cry for help? As symptom of some separate guilt, which Frau Oberholzer has not been able to voice? Bah, time again to ventilate.

*

We are surrounded. Besieged on all sides. Guard posts everywhere. Father below. God upstairs. The one is exercised by your behavior, the other scrutinizes your inner life. Loud swearing is forbidden, and a silent *Fuck!* is not allowed.

We grow older. Sometimes we carry our fathers to the grave. Even God may become a memory. Anyone who doesn't care to be without Him says cautiously: He lives in every blade of grass.—In any case, by and by, the sentries are withdrawn. We are now left unmolested. And even so, we carry on as before. The master bequeaths the estate to the squire, the squire is unable to shake off the sticky bequest and is subsequently his own master. The squire masters himself. He calls the ability to rule himself freedom. Freely, he does what he has to do. He says: *Grüezi*, Yes, and Amen. As before.

After puberty I cleaved—or clove?—to God's mild side, the merciful, the compassionate. Later, in college, the suspicion arose from time to time that Franz wanted to take some of the weight off God, to liberate Him from His strict and savage being, by simply incorporating this being into himself. Franz amputated God's jussive finger, and transplanted it into his own soul. The consequence was a defused God and a live Franz, implacably controlling himself and others, giving himself a rap on the knuckles for each illicit little impulse. Franz in other words did Jehovah's dirty work for Him. Up above, the kindly one smiles, and down below the moralist sweats, yuck.

So I became a minister.

And soon after a married man.

To begin with, I liked both states, and then I didn't dislike them, and towards the end I performed through gritted teeth. (By the bye, I was gritting my teeth before Kezi entered my life, only so could she even have entered my life.)

Strange: The joyful part of my marriage feels distant from me, as do the fulfilling years of the ministry. It's as though happiness didn't exist for memory. Is the brain ashamed of goodness? Is it only want that etches lasting grooves in our hearts? Why must I force myself to invoke such an early picture of love:

Sunshine, cat hunting in the dew, three trees. Helen asleep. Me standing by the window. Stretching, I am still soft with sleep. I feel doubled, wearing your face, freckled wife. Of course, the birds are singing. Of course, the cat is cleaning herself. And if I had felt empty, I should have been deeply envious of her warm fur.

Why does it feel difficult to me today to own up to the shudder that took me the first time I stood in the pulpit, gulping back sobs, and reading the words of the prophet Micah: "He will subdue our iniquities; and thou wilt cast all their sins into the depths of the sea." Instead, the first thing I see today is this: Honeymoon. The hotel in Kalamata. And Helen's nose, half-peeling and half-burnt by the Greek sun. I said: What a pretty little nose, the colors almost like the evening clouds over the Taygetus mountains.—And Helen makes a playful pout at me, and sashays into the en suite. Then a bloodcurdling scream, and I rush in, she's staring at the tub, eyes wide with terror, claws my arm with her nails, trembling and ghostly pale. I laugh. The thing scrabbling about in the tub is nothing worse than a black beetle. I laugh. And Helen wails: I won't stay another hour in this horrible hotel.—I laugh again. She starts pounding at me with her fists. And scratches my face. I push her away and yell: You worrywart!—She huffs into the bedroom, flings herself onto the bed, and goes from one crying jag to the next. I stay in the bathroom, first applying disinfectant to the scratch on my cheek, then seeing to the beetle. I perch on the edge of the bath and briefly consider divorce. And think: The woman's hysterical. And a little later I say to her: I'm sorry.—She sobs: So am I.—Giddy conciliation ritual. Nine months later, a Kalamata baby, our straw-blond Salome.

I understand today—with hindsight—two things: There is a little-publicized reverend's remorse that sooner or later will find you, plunging the victim into almost such stabbing horror as the discovery of gonorrhea. I call it *taedium crucis*. Abruptly, on the fourth or fifth step up to the pulpit, you stop, feel yourself shaken for seconds on end by a violent spasm of disgust, and the next moment you understand: service-aversion, good news overdose. With thick, leathery tongue you sing and chant and sermonize, struggling for devotion, all the while listening in consternation as from a great distance to your daffy babble.

Many times I open my eyes early on a Sunday morning, and feel limitless gratitude that my ministry and my marriage are both behind me.

I slip into my green robe. A little burst of Vivaldi. Coffee with freshly baked croissants. A first, a second, a third cigarette. No more high voice calling out: Schnäggli, don't forget your dog collar.—And never again will the pulpit steps creak under my weight.

On Sunday mornings I have been known to call myself a lucky so-and-so. Breakfast is enjoyed without any impending obligations. No one forces me to roof over a dilapidated sentiment with hypocrisy. Sunday is a gift. It's a day for the character which all week has been socially engaged to recover. Attention needs an occasional pause, and philanthropy has every reason to clamor for a little lie-in. One should listen to this voice, and not straightaway conclude one is deficient in goodness. Occasional selfishness is far less deleterious to the character than that routine benevolence which we come to expect in the social professions, minister, teacher, doctor, and so forth. Loving-kindness needs to remain a hobby, otherwise it acquires something oleaginous. This is the case with all forms of social engagement, it only works if its exercise is unprofessional and discontinuous.

In a word, my Sunday mornings are sacred to me. From time to time, there is a woman keeping me company, that's almost inevitable. In spite of the Kezi calamity, I have remained erotically interested, even if—since the Kezi calamity—I have tended to meet women a little coolly, and prefer to define a relationship in advance as an episode. Most women respond well to that, sometimes so well that I'm not just surprised, but a little hurt. Unlike the woman, the man isn't used to being objectified as an airy, joy-bringing morsel on the side, and feels he alone is entitled to take occasional sexual refreshment. At around forty-five, it dawned on me: Women too are able to appreciate limits; they aren't always avid for the serious consequences with which the theology of love blends if not punishes pleasure-seeking.

To have and to display a liking for the untrammeled is on the one hand unseemly, and on the other displays a cultural nonchalance that one ought properly to admire: Ever since Plato, the fleeting, the temporary, has been accounted soulless, and what are bodies, desire, and pleasure if not fleeting. Soul—the quintessence of duration—inheres only in what is lasting, for which reason Christianity, following in the wake of Platonism, only tolerates the act of love in the context of a stable marriage. Nowadays, the progressive theologian allows true love (in place of marriage). He says: The desire for permanence is in its nature, and, so saying, gilds a thing that lasts about half an hour.

I am neither a zoologist nor a historian. Hence, I am unable to say just when the act ceased to be self-validating, at what point, in other words, it became ambitious, at what point the desire seized it to become expressive and to see itself as the indicator of an emotional vibration. Anyway, the autonomy of the flesh that we may witness in dogs and in the monkey house is over. A visa requirement has been introduced: love. Complicated love. On the one hand set up as a barrier to unbridled lust, on the other as a free pass for pleasure and a guarantee that it—pleasure—can function without conscience spasms, supposing that it is working in the legitimate service of something altogether nobler.

Nothing against love, faithfulness, marriage. Nothing against duration and quality. As a human being and a Swiss, I'm in favor of all that. Only, it's not much of a draw. And my enjoyment is the more unimpaired when I'm not made to think of the headache after. The calculated binge is not in my nature. A dutiful kiss that puts me in mind of the following morning's phone call is not my favorite. That doesn't make me a monster, does it? In the end everyone has a desire for simplicity, and everyone knows the wish for the inconsequential and turns chartreuse with envy when he watches other mammals at it. He can feel: That's what I call unencumbered, there the baroque counts for little, there you don't hear the future's stomach growling in the present.

*

My throat.

I'm choked.

And yet all I did was stress: Not a word against love, faithfulness, marriage. Not a breath! Only, all three are a little bit complicated, hence the notion of the inconsequential has its appeal.

All I meant to say was this: I like being on my own on Sunday mornings. The fridge purrs. If I'm in a particularly good mood, then I'll tune in to the Reformed Evangelical sermon on the wireless. Extraordinary. Extraordinary that I once used to talk like that. I feel myself blushing, the vocabulary causes me to shake, the syntax hurts me, the tone is insufferable. Bitterly, I listen and sometimes I even childishly and eruptively heckle. And yet all along I know: My nausea is directed towards me, only me. For years I was in an abusive relationship with language, producing nothing but smoke, nothing but dingdong merrily on high.

My father was a reluctant churchgoer all his life. Our mother's weekly wish that he accompany her to Mass he generally declined, only when it was her birthday did he consent, get grumpily into his wedding suit, and trail six feet in her wake, as though she had him on a string. He would, though, often listen to the Sunday sermon on the radio. When they got to the Lord's Prayer, he would take his hands out of his trouser pockets and mutter along. Then he would switch off the radio, get up, and say: Ach-men.

How I used to love that word.

Maybe alienation is a law of nature. Maybe it's a mistake that I can't grasp distance except as a manifest truism. And more than likely it's way past time I buried all this father drama anyway.

He was an idiot.

My father was an idiot.
Narrow-minded stupid curmudgeon.
Hard son of a bitch.
Gloommonger.

I'm sorry: I got out of breath.
I'd like to take that back.

6

I WONDER if it'll work another time. We had her inseminated on the sixth of October, two weeks ago, it cost forty
francs and it may not have taken, if it hasn't I'm putting you
down for the butcher. If that's the way you are, a sterile cow
with poor performance and an appetite like a crocodile, then
no farmer on earth can afford you. If you're getting on, then
you're not young anymore, that's the way it is, isn't that so,
Linda, and yet I'm fond of you, and I don't want to give you
away. I'm an old fellow myself, but I'm tough, and without
my roomatizzy and my stupid bladder I'd be someone to
reckon with, and not long ago Therese Mesmer said to me:
Klemens, I declare, you've got more man about you than
some fifty-year-olds I could mention.—All right, I say, and
she says, Swear to God.—I don't know what she's after, probably nothing, I don't want anything myself, all that's finished
with now, on the whole. I was fifty-nine when I lost Gret,
and since then, strange to say, I've been practically becalmed.
Lost the capacity for joy. Sometimes I think maybe I did
inherit my father's condition, it must be in me somewhere,
else Paul could never have inherited it. Since our Anna died,
Paul got it, and ever since he's had to spend three or four
weeks at a time in the asylum, three or four times a year.
They say half the time he's noisy and obstreperous and high
as a kite, and then he has a crash, he's ashamed of himself,

and he crawls into corners. He's got a job in forestry, where thank God they understand him and there's never a word about sacking him. If he's doing well, or rather when he's relaxed and motivated, he goes around with a rucksack and talks and kids around with all sorts of people, visits acquaintances, writes loads of letters, and grabs the breasts of total strangers. That's when you have to get him, which isn't easy, because he's so strong. Maybe a wife would give him what he needs, a bit of support, but what can you do, he's always resisted. When he turned twenty-eight, I said to him: You ought to get married, Paul, it would do you good, and it's what people do. Paul said: I can't, Dad.—Why can't you? I said. Doesn't Vreni want you then? Paul said: She wants me, all right, but I don't want *her* anymore.—I say: Why not, and since when? He says: Since a week.—I see, I say, so this past week you went off her. Might I ask why? He says: That's none of your business. I say: God, I'm hardly squeezing it out of you.—All right, he says, I'll tell you, and be quick about it. Last Sunday I went round there, and she made dinner for me, rice, meat, and vegetables.—He falters, and I say: So, you didn't like her food, she can't cook, is it that?— Paul says: Nonsense, listen to what I'm telling you, after eating I run to the loo, and in the bowl, in the middle of a big puddle of pee is a socking great ... Paul stops, I ask: What? He says: Well, you know, her doings.—I see, I say, her doings, and was that it?—Yes, Paul says sadly, that's it, romance's gone down the drain.—I say: Are you crazy, are you proposing to not let women take dumps, then?—He says: If you'd been there to smell it.—I say: It tends to smell about the same, yours and hers and mine and everyone's.—Right, he says, and that's what I can't accept.

From that day forth, I knew that there was something

wrong with Paul. One year after Anna's death he was put in the asylum for the first time. In March, he went to a pub in town, where he crawled under a table and bit the landlady in the foot, the police were sent for, and they had him put away. All that was on a Wednesday. He was born on a Wednesday too. They used to say: Wednesday's child is full of woe, and maybe there's something to it. My father never started the haying on a Wednesday, whatever the forecast said. And he always gave away Wednesday's calves, they don't prosper, he said, they're unlucky. The minister rolled his eyes, he said that's pure superstition, but the farmers reckoned: He's all right, his vicarage isn't about to get foot-and-mouth. Anyway, Vreni, Paul's intended, got engaged to someone else in a hurry. Curiously, her new feller's name was Paul as well. And just as soon as she's engaged to the other Paul, my Paul rediscovers his love for Vreni. For a while she lets them both pay court to her, and then she chooses Paul #2, who was a well-known sportsman at the time, a soccer star. Ever since, soccer has been a red rag to my Paul, twice he's wrecked a TV set in a public bar, just because they were showing a soccer game. And again, they picked him up, and took him away. I don't like to say it out loud, but in that respect I can understand him. TV is a bane of existence, and sports are a bane of existence, there's nothing anyone can say, that's the truth. A man's reduced to staring, he stops thinking, he sits there gawping like a vegetable. Everyone these days grows up in front of screens, and what are they exposed to? I don't care to have one myself, but Gaudenz does, and Gaudenz says there's only ever three things on it: Either it's sports, or it's blue murder, or it's about getting your whites clean and cat food and so forth.—And that's kept on the whole time our kids are growing up. Which is another reason why I

don't see much of my daughter anymore, my Myrta, because
I can't stand it. We sit down at the table to eat. We are served.
It used to be Grandad first, today it's the kids, well, whatever.
Food is doled out. They yell: Want more!—Mama gives them
more. They guzzle half of it, then they push their plates away,
and they say, Bye, and they scatter off to the idiot box, that's
the way it is these days. Myrta, I tell her, what kind of manners have they got? And Myrta says: Listen, Dad, that's our
business, not yours.—And I think to myself: Say what you
like, but I think it's terrible. What Gaudenz says applies to
the radio too, you can tune it to any station, and it's sports,
sports, and more sports, nothing about farming, nothing
about ordinary people. You can do what's required of you
for a whole lifetime, get up at four a.m. every day, milk cows,
fork manure, and all the rest of it, don't think you'll ever be
on the radio. Whereas if you're a soccer player, you can be
as thick as mince, and you shoot a goal in some international
or other, then you'll be world-famous in seconds, and everyone will be talking about you, and the president himself will
congratulate you, so bursting with pride he'll cack himself.
Whereas you can struggle all your life, raise kids, look after
the farm, get elected to the council and the school board,
take your turn in the fire brigade, as lifeguard, hunting su-
pervisor, and gravedigger, no one on God's sodding earth
will pay you a blind bit of notice, not one newspaper or one
radio will mention you, you are nothing. One measly goal
will bring you more money and fame than an entire working
life, one goal, and humankind will celebrate you, which says
everything about the condition of it, it is and remains crippled and wrecked to its bones and as hollow as oat straw.
And the people who make their living on this warm dungheap and who thanks to human stupidity come to money

and power and do all they can to extirpate what remains of common sense, they are the very worst, and I wish them a thousand devils.

Twice a day I hunker here pressing my forehead against their bellies, and milk, but does that mean I am blind to what's going on outside? I see what I see, and no one can pull any wool over Thalmann's eyes, not West nor East, it's all the same in any case, Yanks and Russkies, Tom, Dick, or Harry, all the same interchangeable wretches, Holy Rollers to the marrow and fake as gibbet wood. Whoever has lived for fifty, sixty, or seventy years and can't get his head around who's in charge of the planet and who's conniving to blow it up should have four more holes drilled in his butt instead of the eyes and ears he doesn't need and doesn't use. I often think: Is it possible that there are people who follow this ghastly mess day in day out without noticing that the so-called superpowers are ten times as stupid as any one of my calves? I'm surprised people still exist who swallow what's put to them, who allow themselves to be whipped up into hatred and stupidity, and who can oh so easily be put into that state of fear that assumes an enemy behind every bramblebush and a tank behind every ashheap. Admittedly, and this is as well, there are still a few people who call a spade a spade, and I have never understood why *they're* called gullible and naive and easily manipulated, but that's what it keeps saying in the papers. I'm happy about each peaceable cow in my cowshed that doesn't lash out or turn its horns on me, what's supposed to be so bad about that? Sure, the journalists have all got degrees and they're seven times smarter than Thalmann here, who just says: Be happy with anyone who's opposed to the damned arms race.

When I'm sitting in the Lamb, which is rare enough these

days, with the other shooting club seniors, and we talk about these matters, then I always say what I think, and they always counter: You old pinko, you, wouldn't you fight for your wife and children when the Russkies invade?—I say: My wife's dead, as you know, and the children are grown-up, and third, I ask you, Titus, where did you do your service in the Second World War, where were you posted?—And Titus says: I've got a bad back, as you know, I was excused service.— I see, I say, you were excused, and what about you, Theo, where were you?—And Theo says: In the Bernese Jura.—I see, I say, in the Bernese Jura, and where were your wife and children at that time?—And Theo says: Back then they were living in Thurgau, on the German border.—On the German border, I say, how interesting, so you're playing cards in the Jura, and your dear ones were living in terror on the German frontier, and yet you say you were defending them.—I was defending the Fatherland, says Theo, we would have held the Alps, I swear, Hitler would have bitten his teeth out there.—I say, Oh yes, the Alps, right, as long as there's one little flag waving on some snowy summit, then a man feels free, even if his dear ones in the green lowlands are long since lying under the rubble.—Oh, stop it, says Theo, stop your nonsense, I don't want to hear any more about it. When I think of what a fabulous marksman you used to be, and what bilge you talk in your old age, it makes my hair curl.— Ooh, Theo, this I must see! calls the landlady, and everyone whinnies with laughter, including me, even though I feel glum and wretched.

It's true, I did use to be a good shot, I had eagle eyes and a steady hand and an unerring sense of the alignment of rear sight and front sight, and even in training I shot better than all my comrades, and yet I didn't feel happy for a single hour in all that time, Lord knows why. Then one day, it must be sixty years ago now, a senior officer said something to me that stuck and will continue to preoccupy me till the day I die. At lunchtime in the canteen, I buy myself a cream puff and carry it in my left hand along the seemingly unending unlit corridor at the end of which is the toilet, where I plan to eat the thing in peace. From about thirty paces, I see the door open and a man comes towards me, an officer. I think: Uh-oh, I'd better salute him, here goes, and of course my right hand makes to shoot up to my cap brim. Then a second thought hits me: Damn, that's the hand with the cream puff. A third thought comes along: In cases like this, we learned in training, it's enough to nod, so dip your head and give the nice officer a nod. All right, so that's what I do. We pass each other in the corridor, I nod, he nods, and I think to myself: Bravo, Thalmann, that's what I call presence of mind. After some fifteen paces, I hear a loud voice behind me: Since when do you not salute an officer?—I stop, turn around, look down at my hands and see that my cream puff is not in my right hand at all, but my left. So the right would have been available for purposes of saluting, but how do I explain all that? I take a couple of steps towards the officer and say: Beg pardon, sir, I thought I was carrying this here in my right hand, now I see that it was in my left all along, and so, and so—He interrupts, shouting in an angry voice: Before you start talking to me, I want you to present yourself properly. Who the hell are you?—Captain, sir, Recruit Thalmann.— He says: Louder.—I call out, Recruit Thalmann, Captain!— He says: Not the foggiest idea of rank, have you. Am I a captain?—I gulp, and walk a little closer, four or five paces, and squinny at his hat, and see that it's not got three skinny lines on it, but three thick yellow ones, which makes him a

colonel. I stammer: Beg pardon, Colonel, sir, I thought…
You had your head at a slight angle, and from where I'm
standing, or rather from where I was standing a moment
ago, it looked as though your hat had the three *narrow*
stripes.—The colonel stares at me in just the way the French
farmer stared at me two years before, he stares at me, and
then in this soft, sympathetic voice he says: Oh, I see, one or
two bulbs short are we, a little bit dim. Do you know what
I mean?—I say: Not quite.—And he says: Exactly, dismissed.

I've forgotten nothing, nothing at all. The butcher said:
You little shit. The farmer said: You're the devil. My uncle
said: What's going to to become of you? The colonel said: A
little bit dim. And a few years before that, the teacher said:
You wretched little squirt, the Almighty will punish you.—
That was Christmas, I was maybe ten at the time. The teacher
said: All right, children, today we're going to do something
very special, we're going to draw Christmas cards together,
and each card is going to have a Christmas wish on it. What
do you think would be nice? What shall we write on our
cards? Here's the chalk, anyone with an idea for a nice Christmas wish, come up to the board and write it.—The class
thinks and groans, but no one steps up. Is that really so hard,
says the teacher, Make an effort or else it's get your arithme-
tic books out and continue where we left off on page forty-
four.—Suddenly I feel the impulse, I raise my arm and I
walk up to the front and I write on the board: Happy Easter.—The teacher first turns pale, then red, and then he gets
his paddle out, and he gives me fifteen on each hand and he
screams: You wretched little squirt, the Almighty will punish you.

Heigh-ho. And looking back today, I'm bound to say: the
Almighty didn't do me any favors. There are people who are

pursued by good fortune, whose sawbuck even brings forth young, well, I'm not one of them, the Almighty didn't do me any favors, I didn't have an easy life, and when my father died when I was twelve, I was thinking: This is what I get for writing Happy Easter. In '46 I buried him, the teacher, he got to be old, which is to say about as old as I am now, I shoveled his grave, and I thought to myself: Rather a living squirt than a dead teacher. All in all, though, I forgave him, and because he used to tell us all the time to be sure to drink elderberry juice, I planted an elderberry on his grave against all the regulations, and that elderberry's still doing well, it's outlived his grave. Fotsch was his name, Hans or Eugen Fotsch, I don't remember.

No, I don't forget a thing, I was on the council then, and my pals shook their heads and said: Klemens, this is a bad idea, there'll be bad blood in the village, cut down that elderflower and plant an evergreen instead, you can't have a councilor in breach of cemetery regulations.—I said, Very well, then, you can find yourselves a new gravedigger, and I'll give up my seat on the council as well.—You're as stubborn as a mule, says Manz, and the late Hänny says: Good God, where's it going to end, a cemetery's no place for an elderflower.—I say: You owe it to Fotsch that you can read and write and do sums, and you won't even let him have a flowering bush.—He used to smack us, says Mosimann. I say: And so says you, even though when we're round at the Lamb after a meeting, it's always you lamenting that the young teachers just go ahem! ahem! and haven't the least idea of physical punishment!—Oh, give over, says Mosimann, either way, that bush has got to go.—I say: Please yourself, only whatever you do: mind how you go.

And the upshot was they didn't do anything. Fotsch kept

his shrub, which is still flourishing, and when there's a June burial, the mourners stand around the cemetery sniffing and saying: What's that heavenly smell?—I'll admit, I didn't stick up for the shrub just for Fotsch's sake, I've had a close affinity to elderflower for several reasons. When I was a nipper, my father told me: Look here, Menzli, that bush over there, between field's edge and forest, that's an elderflower, which is a sacred plant, and whoever does anything to hurt it will be horribly punished, it's always been the way of it, so watch out, and if you pick its berries, make sure you don't hurt it.—I never forgot that, and at the beginning of July '31, five weeks before the wedding, I took Gret to a different bush, which was an elderflower as well, and up in the sky was a full moon and down below the wretched scent of the blossoms, well, guess what, that's where we made Paul, our very first time, that's got to be more than just a coincidence.

So then, Linda, I really wonder if you'll make it, for me all those insemination fees add up, and without calves I think you're a bit costly. You take my time and my money, and I wangle around on your old titties, kneading and squeezing and stripping, and if all you offer me is three liters, I have to say, your chances are not looking good.

7

PAUL TRULY is an elderflower baby. I have my sources. My old auntie Klär is still alive, who since the death of her brother can talk to me again, and does so. And more: Every other week she tidies my apartment. I let it happen, even though I feel miserable in tidy rooms. I let it happen, because she talks to me while she cleans. There's very little she doesn't know. She knows so much about my father that she leaves little room for the imagination.

My ultimate aim is understanding, which is to say relief, a kind of twofold relief: At the moment of true comprehension both the inquirer and the party inquired into heave a deep sigh. I operate twice over. I show myself to the object as I approach it. I call out from a distance: Look, this is me approaching!—The object of the inquiry will only disclose itself to the naked inquirer. If *he* shows himself, then it will permit *itself* to be seen. Such is my uncontemporary belief.

But for the moment, my throat is still acting up.

My second source: Titus Feusi. A resident of the same retirement home as Auntie Klär. They have known one another since infancy. Recently ashamedly inflamed in some late-onset passion. He too knows a lot. Whatever she doesn't know, he, the great sitter in bars, knows, who alone, as he says, was able to flush the discreet Klemens out of his bush.

In a word, I am not blathering here, and if I were, then it would be my affair.

So Paul genuinely is an elderflower baby. This matters to me. I summarize: Five weeks before the wedding, my father loses self-control. A bit of a floral whiff, and morality is out the window. I know that and understand it, but would have you know: This never happened to me with my wife, not with Helen, not with us. It was understood by both of us that we would save the ultimate and highest for when we were married. Lying together, and so on. Well, perhaps it's not the actual thing, perhaps it's only long forbearance that turns it into that—no, no, that's not right, the actual thing is a given and always beyond doubt, otherwise one's forbearance would be neither needful nor meritorious.

I was told about the birds and bees in confirmation camp. I was fifteen. The technical side was kept short, but I understood it. The minister demonstrated it with the aid of a glove, slipping it on and off, described it as a divine gift, and said by way of conclusion: Keep yourselves clean.

Recently, a rather cultivated client of mine remarked that sex is only really enjoyable with Catholic women; their sense of sin makes them especially passionate and lends spice to their embraces. He says it's wrong to attack received morality; in fact, it should be placed under protection, because— when used scientifically, in the manner of an ingredient—it guarantees the best results. You mustn't, so my customer instructs me, you mustn't think morality is a precept. The point of morality isn't ethical behavior, but the exciting sensation of being extra sinful. Since this feeling is inhibiting as well as stimulating, you are required to mobilize all your resources to overcome your inhibition, your resistance; and in the process develop an extraordinary strength of feeling, and so guilt can generate proper passion. For which reason I favor moralistic women.

My dear Herr Jakobi, I reply irritably, what you say may make a little sense in the context of the general idiocy of our lives. But not much. And anyone who so calculatedly and pleasurably comes to an accommodation with perversion has no business in my practice. So, if you please!

Jakobi says: You are a fanatic, and I like you, we have much to learn from one another. You fight against conventional morality on behalf of a mysterious ethics, while I undermine it and place it at the service of pleasure—of which you are also in favor. You demolish, I renovate; you clear away, I repurpose.

I haven't been able to shake Jakobi off. He's been coming for the past seven weeks, and gabbles the hour away. When I ask him what his trouble is, and what prompted him to seek me out, he just shrugs his shoulders and says: Search me, you're the expert.

Of course I know what it is. As a "nocturnal silver lion," Herr Jakobi has been flitting through the reports of Fräulein Trüssel, of whom I am also an admirer, but more of that later.

Anyway, back in the day, Helen and I, we waited. She came from a religious background and was perhaps a little slow, as indeed was I. Once, maybe three weeks before the wedding, I said as a joke—I even said it in English—Come on, baby, let's do it.—It flopped. She was aghast and said: Now, Franz, that was a tasteless thing to say.—(She generally preferred to call me Schnäggli.)

Helen was rarely amused.

I see us both on our honeymoon again. We are sitting in the back of a taxi taking us from Kalamata to Sparta. Ahead of us, imposing, rough, and dry, the Taygetus range. I am pressing your hand and saying: Isn't this awe-inspiring.—You reply: I think it's hot and bumpy myself.—Just then our Greek takes his foot off the gas, turns right up a track that's about half the width of the car, and after a few yards, stops. Deafening crickets; smell of wild sage. What's the matter with him? you ask. I say: Probably needs to powder his nose.—But our driver doesn't get out. He turns around, gives me a sheepish grin, points to you with his little finger, then to himself, then through the open window to a clump of purplish flowers, and says: No pay, taxi free, just ficki-ficki.

I exploded. I whooped. The Greek was impressionable and laughed along. You didn't. You sat there, turned to stone. Purple face and livid expression. Then you got out. And before slamming the door, you hissed: Vulgarians, the pair of you.

There could be no question of driving on with this particular taxi. He seemed to get it, and just shrugged a shoulder regretfully. I mutely handed him his drachmas, and took off after you. We wandered silently in the general direction of Sparta. You pulled your hand away from mine, another occasion for me to register your flair for making me feel guilty. Eventually, we managed to speak. You spoke of human dignity. I take your laughter, you said, as a form of displaced complicity with that scumbag.

I agreed with you.

At that time, I couldn't take disharmony.

We yomped for four hours. Finally, a Danish couple in a VW bus picked us up and gave us a lift to Sparta. Up in our room, you showed me, with no commentary, a small blister on your foot, I forget which one.

I almost apologized again.

I am not that much given to superstition. And yet, and yet . . . On the morning of my wedding, things transpired that, with hindsight, might have been interpreted as warnings. When I wake up, my right ear is completely blocked. Nada. A dull whooshing sound. Horrid. Why today of all days? I ask aloud, hear a distant impression of my voice, and straightaway feel like an invalid. I get up. I tweak like a maniac at my earlobe. Then a shower, to try and clear the blockage. Nothing.

Miserable breakfast. The phone rings. I pick up the receiver, can't hear a dickybird, call hello? hello! into it, then switch it to my other ear. Helen seems exasperated, lists everything that needs to be taken care of before noon. I say: My absolute priority is my obstruction.—What obstruction? she asks. Helen, I say, I've got a blocked ear, I'm practically deaf.—She says: I've had about enough of your fusses.

After our phone call I climb up onto a chair and jump down on the floor with my head inclined to the side and landing on my right foot. I do it again and again. Suddenly the door swings open, and my brother Paul with rucksack comes staggering into the room, reeking of booze, and says: I'm looking for my glasses.—Here?—No, not here, I expect they're in the forest somewhere.—And what am I supposed to do about it?—As a good Christian, you will help me find them, I need glasses to find my glasses, it's a tragedy, so come along!—My dear Paul, that's not possible, you know I'm getting married today.—Oh, you're getting married today. Was I supposed to smell that?—Paul, I say exasperatedly, I sent you written and spoken invitations.—Oh, he says, but what about my glasses?—I'm in a rush, Paul, I probably need to go to the doctor, I've got a blocked ear and I'm practically deaf.—And I'm practically blind, he says, where do you think I left them?—I thought you said they were in the forest?—No, he says, that's one place they're definitely not. What made you think they were?—I've had about all I can take! I yell. He says: I can quite understand your being nervous, getting married is no walk in the park, I'm going to go to a chemist's and buy you a rubber pump.

Half an hour later, Paul returned with an ear pump. He filled it with warm water. All right, Franzli, he said, come over here and be a brave boy.—And ten seconds later, I felt born again.

He didn't come to the ceremony. He turned up for the party, late. With rucksack and hiking boots. Half-cut. No glasses. I could sense Helen's embarrassment and the mixture of horror and amusement in the expressions of her relations. Paul danced like a blind baby elephant, stood on the toes of his partners and put paid to the rhythm of the most adept ladies with his garlic breath. When he struck a fork against an empty bottle and rose to speak, even I was a little afraid. He said: My dear couple, in general terms, it doesn't take much to satisfy us. Am I right or am I right? (I nod weakly, Helen sits bolt upright, around us some feeble throat-clearing.) I hope, Paul continues, I hope you manage anyway, and with that I conclude my speech. (Relieved applause.)

No one can believe what happened next. Those who

witnessed it with their own eyes have stopped telling the story, because no one believes them. Paul sat down beside Helen and took her white patent leather clutch, lying beside her dessert plate, for her dessert plate. He helped himself to caramel pudding with whipped cream. All the witnesses looked on transfixed. By the time the first of them squealed, Paul was finished.

Helen did not move a muscle.

Paul was terribly well intentioned, but she shot him a glare through her spectacles. He slunk out. I went after him. I said: Don't be upset, she's just a bit wound up, it's her nerves, you know what women are like.—Paul said: If I were you, I would take that sourpuss back where you found her.

I feel sick. I'm a little disgusted by this anecdote-enriched past. I'm ventilating.

Helen left with our daughters. As they're both asthmatic, they moved to the Alpine foothills. I'm allowed to see them once a year, here in town. I pick them up at the station, we go to a restaurant, and after lunch I take them back to the station. It's my sense they're finding puberty heavy going. They giggle a lot and are snitty and treat me like an old man. Nothing about them seems mine. Eva was four when we divorced, and Salome a couple of years older. I don't know what they know about my life, presumably Helen doesn't tell them much. I can't take myself seriously as a father anymore. It's time I put an end to these annual rituals, which are becoming increasingly disagreeable.

*

I am not solitary. But I do look forward to the post in the morning.

I would have nothing against seeing Helen again. Her hatred has had the better part of eleven years to run its course; you would think by now we could manage a conversation. She doesn't even know that I'm the most devoted reader of the occasional articles she writes for the newspaper. She likes to review new literary publications, thus returning to an earlier hobby she was kept from pursuing by all the duties she had as a minister's wife. I always enjoyed reading book reports. The fact that in a time when everything is relativized people can still be found to say this is good, this is bad, I find fascinating. Helen speaks her mind. I almost learned more about her than about the books she was writing about. Of course, she doesn't just blurt out her reasons for liking or disliking a thing, or what her standards are. That is neither customary nor necessary and it would infringe on her personal freedom. So, of course, she would never write: My dream man must be active and manly and know his mind.— Instead, she writes: One begins to wonder when the current vogue for flaccid antiheroes will finally come to a stop.

Over time, I've made the following discovery: Those books that Helen rejects are the ones I find especially interesting. They are subversive, making clear that their authors, in writing them, did so to avoid doing something far worse. These are the books that crackle subtly, the semi-house-trained powder kegs of books, the incautious, unconsidered, and if you like erroneous ones, and Helen doesn't care for them. They make her come over all maiden-auntish and offended.

She is looking to be confirmed, not menaced. Which is where we differ. Being petted just puts me to sleep.

So, albeit as an anonymous reader, I remain in contact with Helen, and am attentive to the least variations in her values. There is no indication of any softening, and hence no real change. Helen was always narrow and dogmatic and inelastic; nothing springy could hope to meet with her favor. Today, it seems clear to me that her static quality could not but make a rebel of me, and that it was she who dynamized me.

The accused countersues. If only to exculpate himself, Franz blames Helen. The guilty party is gladdened by any defect in his victim. The sum of all her shortcomings makes him the true victim, just as, the obverse, the glaring inadequacies of the victim seem almost to make her the culprit.

Should I leave the frog to believe his abode here is a swamp? Am I not justified in justifying myself, have I not the right to point out the contingency of every action? Ye gods—as if there were such a thing as a misstep in a vacuum. I've got Kezi leading, Helen bringing up the rear, and in the middle Franz with his brains and balls and past conditioning. That makes five factors at each other's throats, each one pushing and pulling and choking for advantage, but one's making the running. Then all that's left is Franz's naked deed, denounced by self-righteous onlookers, the people who always talk about free will when it's others quitting the strait path, and themselves, by sheer luck, behaving.

I don't want to exculpate myself. I have a lot of time for free will, and from time to time I believe in such a thing, and in my guilt, damnit, but do I have to crawl around on my hands and knees for the rest of my life, do I have to turn self-laceration into a *raison d'être*?

I promise you one thing, though: One day I'll be sitting under a grapevine, or maybe a fig tree. I'll draw deep and satisfying breaths through my shamelessly open mouth, and the sun will warm my tonsils, and no one will stop me. You'll be lying off to the side in the grass, still just about wiggling, but little more than a corpse.

For the moment, though, I'm still at my desk in my apartment. Outside, there's December rain and nighttime traffic, which I don't mind. It's no bad thing to be reminded of the outside world occasionally. Not because I'm displacing it, or because I'm sufficient unto myself, not at all. If we took the mouse as our representative of the outside world, then I'd be the buzzard, coming down and grabbing it, hauling it off to a quiet place and eating it. I don't have a very patient relationship to the outside world. Instead, I'm inclined to gobble it up, so that things—in a slow ferment—lie heavily inside me, almost forcing me to contemplation. As soon as the outside is inside, I wake up. Am I a master of the posthumous joke? A ruminant? In any case, reality takes time to betray its gristly nature, becomes, in its disintegration, my partner. If I were a painter, I would stand in the landscape without a paintbrush. Shyly and fleetingly, I'd catch an eyeful and carry it—said landscape—home with me, and lie on the sofa with it quietly until it whispered in my ear: All right, I'm ready now, fetch the canvas.

The buttoned-up bits of reality, gulped down in spite of myself, are softened up in my internal juices, become malleable and flexible and accept my will.

I understand that such imagery is not up to the task, and that the metaphor of digestion has limits. So let me put it more briskly: I'm a Romantic. And that's why the sound of cars does me good—why even the furniture polish in the vicarage in the end did me good. Even the horrendous fact that Helen would swab the toilet seat three or four times a day with a damp cloth and a strange reverence, even that wasn't a deal-breaker. Because then there would have been nothing but assimilable things, and in time we would forget about the existence of the outside world, and the very idea of unpalatability would fade.

I'll be fifty soon and I wonder what being grown-up will feel like. Was I grown-up when I turned twenty-two? For a bet, then, I ate a coffee cup. No problem. My stomach was equal to the challenge. Today, I poke at my sauerkraut. An un-grown-up way of behaving, only confirming one's suspicion that being grown-up, like everything else, is a passing condition. Admittedly, there are sixty-year-olds who cope with everything, and seventy-year-olds who make their way up to the high board and—everyone looking away—dive. But all in all, being grown-up seems to fade, the ability to cope with cold and wet weakens, and our old early sense of threat returns. To the post-adult, many things are intolerable, and more that seem impenetrable to him turn up all the time, exacerbating his sense of alienation: What am I doing in a world that daily grows by a million more things I don't understand, and that complicates itself by facts and arguments that remain mysterious to me? What do I know about microelectronics beyond the flicker? Who can still adjust and define himself in a slew of riddles? Who can resist a

sense of impotence, and what with? Who can stave off im-
becility and why?

Thus the post-adult, almost desperately, while the grown-
ups frown and exchange glances.

Let me tell you something, frog, take it as my confession. At
the very dawn of my career as a counselor was a deception.
You will of course call it a wicked con. But let me remind
you, this is a competitive business, and everyone tries hard.—
I liked Fräulein Trüssel, and Fräulein Trüssel liked me. From
the outset. She didn't care about pleasing me, which pleased
me. I only noticed the blackheads on her nose when she
pointed them out to me, and told me she purposely wasn't
doing anything about them.—I'm a Virgo, she said, almost
aggressively, in our first session. To which I replied: Pleased
to meet you, I'm a late Aquarian myself.—She says: Inclined
to the fantastical, volatile, and full of curiosity.—I say: Correct, but we're here to talk about you. Inclined to the me-
thodical, very tidy, very clever, although Mercury represses
your emotions, makes you cool, erotically hard to arouse,
which might make you think of yourself as frigid.

I was talking partly off the top of my head, partly because
I had once read such stuff in a magazine somewhere, partly,
to be sure, from inspiration. She sat down, took me in with
her large eyes (green), and in a hoarse voice said: Correct.
When someone touches me, I shudder. I always meet the
wrong man. I think there are only wrong men. The throaty
chuckle. Crude beforehand and crude afterwards, and in
between they're mechanical and doggish. The possessive
paws on my sit-upon. The cold sweat. The slimy arrogance.
The donkey prick lurking inside the most seemingly sensitive.

The most disgusting of all was the last one. Tied me up and afterwards kept proclaiming: The silver lion leaves the site of his triumphs.—Would you call that normal, Herr Thalmann?

By no means, Fräulein Trüssel, but I expect your abhorrence is also outside the normal range.

What do you think I see, Herr Thalmann, when I look back on the sample of males I have had dealings with?

Tell me.

A caravan of bristly fools. A noisy phallopathic mafia.

We are not here—or not yet—to discuss Fräulein Trüssel, and in fact the only reason I mention her is because I'm making my confession. It was she who slipped me the information I required for the alluded-to stunts in my early days as a counselor. Her astrology obsession gave me the idea.

For instance, one Herr Hommel came to me for counseling, Joseph Hommel. No sooner had we hung up than I picked up the receiver again, called the canton passport office, asked to speak to Fräulein Trüssel, who worked there in a secretarial capacity, and said: Good morning, I have a question for you regarding one Hommel, Joseph. Is he on your books?—She said, Hold on a minute, and then: Born in Lüterkofen, Canton Solothurn, on November 9, 1929, police constable.—Thank you! I say, and she says: Anytime.

And then I prepare myself thoroughly. Four days later I have the man himself in my office. I look at him for a while. Herr Hommel, I finally say, I take you to be a man of uncommon willpower and combativeness, you don't seem to me to be in the habit of coming for advice?

Correct. This is my first time.

Then I expect the matter you've come to me regarding is accordingly grave.

You could say so.

Might it be to do with your prostate complaint, or possibly your bladder?

Good God, how on earth do you know?

Herr Hommel, the genitourinary system is so to speak the Achilles' heel of the Scorpio. And I hardly think you'd be anything but a Scorpio. Mars is all too evident, but you're no Aries, because the form of your skull indicates an autumn birthday. Which leaves only Scorpio, probably second decade, a November birthday, perhaps the eighth or the tenth, though I'm sticking my neck out here.

Herr Hommel clears his throat and says: That's wild, I never had any time for that nonsense. You reckon the eighth or the tenth, well, you're not far off, it's the ninth.

Now, you can stop your croaking, it never did any harm to anyone, on the contrary, by means of a tiny miracle I restored a measure of faith, because without that any therapy is doomed. I created a climate of trust in which my client could feel transparent—perhaps even understood.

The positive initial response, admittedly, was in part based on trickery; but it did wonders for the therapy, and even the client's welfare. And hence mine as well: My stock soared, and my financial anxiety—because once defrocked, I was facing ruin—abated. Instead, my practice was soon bursting, so that very soon I was able to quit the hocus-pocus and no longer required the services of Fräulein Trüssel.

That's all it was, frog, you see, you've got me in such a twist that even perfectly unexceptionable conduct seems to require confessing.

Could it be that that's the immature element in me?

At night—even now—I often have the fear of being a scoundrel. I wake up and feel inundated with suspicions. A sudden sense of wickedness plunges me into a panic, instantly extinguishing all the lighter parts of my sense of self. I feel completely alien to myself and would implicitly believe anything about me that a stranger might say. I'd also be prepared to see that credulity as a moral weakness and as proof that I lack a center, a moral kernel. And, conversely, I wouldn't be disinclined to believe that it was evidence of richness and a suggestion that I contain multitudes. And then I would feel ashamed of such an interpretation.

In the morning, the edges grow back, and when he stands in front of the mirror, Franz knows full well whom he is shaving.

An afterword on Joseph Hommel. He killed himself. At the time of his suicide in the detention cell where he was supposed to be sobering up, even though he had only drunk one beer, he had long since ceased to be my client. Nor was he any longer a police constable in any meaningful way. He came down with a lung condition following his prostate operation. Also, he must have found what he was reduced to doing particularly humiliating: checking parking meters.

One July night—no particular occasion, no jubilee, no birthday, just the usual gang at the bar—Hommel was on his way home. Call of nature, maybe, hence the detour through the station underpass. In the gents, Hommel perhaps runs a comb through his hair, takes a sad look in the mirror, thinks: Male-pattern baldness, precancerous polyp growth, erectile dysfunction.

He leaves the gents, rushes through the deserted underpass, passes three phone booths, one of them vandalized, hears a ringing, and stops. It's a fact, the middle phone is ringing. Curious, thinks Herr Hommel. And then, on an impulse, he yanks the door open and shuts it after him, picks up the receiver.

The two policemen descending the flight of stairs from the station platform to the underpass are witness to the following scene: A man standing in the second phone booth, listening for a long time, then speaking, listening again. Then suddenly drops the receiver, stands there trembling, the receiver is gently swinging back and forth, the man lashes out at it, the glass of the phone booth shatters.

The policemen come running up and pull him out of the phone booth, and one of them says: Now we've got the vandal. The other says: Jesus, that's Hommel! Have you gone crazy, Sepp?—Joseph doesn't speak, he's gasping and choking, can't get a word out. The policemen seem anxious, until finally the younger one says: Drunk as a skunk!—The older one says, Joseph, I'm afraid we're going to have to take you back to the station, you know how it is, then you can sleep it off.—And Hommel nods and chokes and nods and he's all gray and on the way he vomits over a parking meter, and he pouts and says in a squeaky voice: Sway sgotta be.—The policemen laugh nervously. Flanking him, they walk a little faster and keep casting anxious glances at Sepp Hommel, who, strangely humming, is reeling towards his catastrophe.

*

An afterword on Fräulein Trüssel. (At her request, I call her *Frau* Trüssel; the suffix -lein, she correctly diagnoses as the linguistic precipitation of male condescension, a pseudo-affectionate diminutive, an unsolicited branding or labeling making it easier for the male world to identify available quarry.) Frau Trüssel, then, was my first. With her I embarked on my career as counselor. With her I suffered my first (semi-) defeat as well: Her disgust with men (inasmuch as they were men and not merely people) was proof against anything, and so all-embracing that she even squirted the hind parts of her bitch, long since "snipped," with an anaphrodisiac spray to ward off pursuing packs.

One thing isn't clear to me, Frau Trüssel, I said at the time. You get involved with men, and call these same men a lustful pack of abusers.

Herr Thalmann, says Frau Trüssel, that's why I'm here, I want you to free me from it.

From your revulsion?

No, no, from my compulsion.

I can't do that, Frau Trüssel. The revulsion I might be able to talk you out of, but the compulsive attraction is usually something you're born with.

But you're all so horribly mucky.

Who is? Me?

No, no, men, they jab their pinkies in their ears, and pull out the wax, which they examine before wiping it on the tablecloth. They waggle their toes in my face and demand my sympathy for their athlete's foot. Disgusting. And then the dandruff. And the stains around their flies. The smoker's breath. And to top everything the butterfingered groping round my bra clasp, and the rest over before you know it—

no, no one can or shall ever rob me of my nausea.—What you're telling me here, Fräulein Trüssel, is indeed unappetizing. So what drives you into the arms of this pack, if it's not desire?

Wrong, wrong, or maybe half-right. My appetite is strong, I'll admit it, but the food is revolting, that's my tragedy.

I say again, Fräulein Trüssel, while the appetite is a gift from mother nature, the food too is what mother nature provides, the best thing we can do is try to master our disgust.

But that has to stay! And there's one thing you're forgetting, Herr Thalmann: One could always dine from a different menu!

How do you mean?

The world isn't just made up of men.

Aha. And what role is there for me there?

But I told you already: I wanted you to free me from men, support me in my desire to switch orientation.

I did so, if with no great enthusiasm. I no longer tampered with Roswitha Trüssel's disgust. And yet there was my pride as a psychologist and as a man, which wouldn't allow me to take this nausea at face value, i.e. to accept it as a valid response to something objectively disgusting. Because some ladies soothe their inner frog by letting it hop around the garden of earthly delights and occasionally take a little nibble here or there, but generally make it clear by constantly turning up their noses that they are there involuntarily and under duress and it doesn't really count.

And secondly: Are women any more appetizing? Ask my brother. If the Almighty hadn't given me such a powerful drive, thus Paul, then faced with those slippery crannies and bulges and furrows I could imagine I'd quail.

This, mind you, is Paul speaking, not me. I will merely say: There was none so lovely as Kezia.

8

Interesting animal, Beth. Maybe not a beauty, a bit on the bony side, and a broken horn, but generally in good nick and a credit to her breed. Also a decent milker, except when there's a foehn on, which she can't help noticing. It's not the only thing she notices either. She doesn't like the vet. As soon as a stranger comes into the shed, she shits. She's on strangely good terms with our Appenzeller, who's forever licking her behind. Makes me wonder what kind of dog does that. Interesting animal, Beth. The only thing that bothers me slightly is your quiet heat. You can't tell when you're in heat, you don't see it and don't hear it, so getting you inseminated is always a bit of a lottery. But if we strike lucky, everything's always tickety-boo, and when her time approaches, I know: You'll calve at the next full moon.

It's like that. There's some things an animal will notice. Compared to a human it picks up on a lot, including a handful that a human wouldn't register at all. Anyone who knows cows knows they're not as stupid as townies think, who don't know a thing about nature, beyond the pot of basil on their balcony. I often think to myself: The townie's kaput, and at the same time he must be fearfully healthy, otherwise he wouldn't stand a chance. Anyone who can endure the noise and the reek and the crush and the dirt indoors and out, and the crowds in the stores and the fighting over parking spots and the madmen running around all over the place, I tell you, anyone who can survive all that has got to be as robust as a snowplow. They're moving out into the country now, the townies are, but usually it ends in tears. They don't adapt, Stüssi doesn't wash the pavement outside his house, not even on Saturdays, Berger hates the sound of cowbells, and just the other day Frau Gallmann said to my Klär: I'd be perfectly happy here, if it wasn't for the manure smell.— I say to Klär: My God, what a gripe, sits there gathering soot and breathing lead tetrachloride, and then when she encounters a natural odor, the stuck-up goose wrinkles her nose at it.—Ach, you know, she's all right really, says Klär, only... —Only what? I say. She says, Oh, never mind.—I say: Come on, out with it.—She says, Oh, it's just the other week I went to take her a little basket of plums, and she says: That's very nice of you, only neither of us especially likes plums.—I took the basket home with me, and I was annoyed with myself, but I thought, so long as people are honest with you.—Honest, I say, honest! Spoiled is what they are, that stupid fruitcake, what would have been honest would be if she'd told you: We think plums are beneath us!—That's the way it really is. To the Gallmanns and the rest of the incomers, a plum's just a wee bit common, what they'd much rather is buy some mirabelles air-freighted from Burma or Peru, costing a franc apiece, money's no object after all, the main thing is you stuff your face with rarities, the main thing is you don't just guzzle plums like your country neighbor. That's how it is today, I'm completely calm about it, I just say to myself: They all shit, and they all die, and I continue: God have mercy on all those spoiled misbegotten prosperous so-and-sos, in case the times ever change! Then Frau Gallmann would come slithering up on her knees rattling with hunger, and beg me for a few plums, and I'd say: Have you heard, they have new sky-blue mirabelles from Peru, why don't you try those?

Myself, I grew up in poverty. Bread soup and potatoes, on Sundays a caraway sausage shared between six of us. I'm not saying that's the way it should be. It was tough. All I'm saying is: It's worse nowadays. A year ago, Klär dragged me along one Saturday to the new shopping center, a vast set of premises on the edge of town, the size of seven football fields, and inside among other things was a vast hall filled to the rafters with about a million things to eat, you can buy anything the earth produces there, all stacked and stored and heaped and displayed, a horrific excess, under garish neon lights, and all the time you're hearing this voice in your ear, dripping onto you like slime, telling you about savings and helping yourself and special offers and multi-packs. But worst of all are the people, almost entirely women, but no, there are men as well, pushing carts ahead of them the size of bathtubs, and filling them up as well. They have the glazed expression of newborn calves, and their hands wander across to the stacks, and pick an item and lay it quickly in their cart. By the time they're standing in the checkout line, they've got their carts full to the brim, at the top is a quicky package of thirty-two loo rolls, and I'm sure they'll get through the lot in a weekend if they eat everything they've bought. Only, they don't eat, they just buy, and come Monday half of it winds up in the bin, that's surely beyond doubt, don't let anyone tell you otherwise. Paul used to be a driver for the town undertaker for a year, and when he gave that up and worked for refuse disposal, he told me: Half a thirty-five-liter sack per person per day, and at the end of ten weeks I couldn't stand it anymore, and people don't produce anything but rubbish, Paul said, and he's right, and that's why I say it's worse today.

What do you expect? they say at the Lamb and Flag, that's prosperity for you, and if people only bought half as much, then the jobs would go, production jobs as well as garbage disposal.—I say: Maybe I'm an old nag that doesn't get anything but oats, but this is how I see it: If someone only buys half the amount as before, then half his wage is enough and half his job too, so the rest will be available for someone else who again will only buy the half and get by on half a wage and half a job, and so on and on.—Ach, you and your pie-in-the-sky calculations, says Mäder, that's all we need, lying about like Africans.—And Titus Feusi says: Then growth and prosperity would be a memory, and anyway, people want every last dime they make.—That's true, says Theo, and just as well, we need industry and we need performance, otherwise we might as well pack up.—I say: If you don't want to see all that's being chucked out and going to waste nowadays, and the crap that's being churned out, and every last thing with reference to saving jobs and creating jobs, then it's your own fault, and I don't mind telling you after six pints: There's no chance of this nation of fat pigs and motions unanimously carried being shrunk, but cheers anyway.—Cheers, Klemens, calls the landlady, here's to a long life and no shrinking!—And they all laugh, and I laugh as well, though I feel godawful.

Paul's right, aside from rubbish people don't produce much that lasts, he is good-hearted, Paul is, and so some people treat him like a child, and some in the pub say: Red hair—no one there, Red opinions, devil's pinions.—It's just like the henyard. As soon as a hen is unlike the rest, as soon as it's sick for instance, then there's no mercy for it, then all the other hens come along and pick on the sick one and bully it and literally peck it to death. Of course, Paul puts up a fight, he's got every right to, but when he loses his temper, he gets thrown out and is banned from the pub for a month. It's not easy for him, though it's better now that he's got the job as a forester, they understand him there. He started off as a trainee butcher after school, that really wasn't his thing. The second week he came home and said: I was on abattoir duty again, and I had to rinse off sixty cows' heads, soften them up in hot water and shave them, in the corner was a pile of skins that kept twitching for hours, I don't want to be a butcher, Dad.—I say: If you begin a thing, you've got to see it through.—He locked himself in the toilet and was up vomiting half the night. The third week, he kept fainting in the abattoir, and the manager rang and said: Will you kindly pick up your son, we've got other things to do than sweet-talk a neurotic kid that'll never make a butcher.—Then he started another traineeship, this time as a cemetery gardener in town, and he finished that successfully, and worked there for three years. Today I think that job wasn't right for him either and poisoned his spirit. Something happened one icy day in November. He was out winterizing graves all morning. At two o'clock there was a ceremony, and Paul said to himself: I'll go sit in the chapel and warm up a bit. Then right at the back of the gallery, sleep got the better of him, and then he starts clicking his tongue very loudly—he always does when he sleeps—and the minister and the mourners got upset and he was fired. Someone in the town administration feels sorry for him, and he's given a job as a driver for the burial institute. That was when he started drinking, four glasses of Tyrolean wine first thing, and he gets in an accident in his hearse, and he's fired a second time. Then he works in garbage disposal for a while, gives that up, does this and that, can't stick it out anywhere, finally he gets this job in forestry, and at last things start to look up for him. They turn a blind eye when he goes walkabout with his rucksack, or when he throws himself at anything in skirts. In the forest they look the other way, but then the townies get ahold of him, and sedate him with injections and pills, and then once he's calm and broken and sad again, they let him go. Myrta's scared of him. He often talks to Myrta when he's excited. There's no need to be scared of your brother, I say to her, he wouldn't hurt a fly. She says: You ought to see him, he comes and babbles and talks our hind legs off, and he tells the children awful stories, then he lies down on the sofa and for three hours he sings, "I'm a hard man, but I've felt the joys of love." Just that one line, again and again, it's impossible to get him to stop, it almost drives *us* mad. Once, I said: If you don't stop now, Paul, I'll call the hospital.—You just try it, little sis, he says, and I go over to the telephone and pick up the receiver, he chases me, and puts the wire in his mouth and bites down on it until he's bitten it clean through, and then he lies down again and goes back to his singing.

That's the way it goes. He needs a wife. Most bachelors are a bit peculiar, especially in their later years. Some turn to drink, others read their Bibles, others again are a deviled egg short of a picnic. My late brother, Gustav, was odd, he failed to grow up, that's right, that's what it is, bachelors refuse to grow up, when he was seventy-four in the home, Gustav was still carrying on like a child, there's truth in the saying: If you remain a calf for thirty years, you'll never be a cow. There was one inmate by the name of Vogler. And this Vogler character used to dole out soup for his table every day, that was his job. Gustav's place is on the same table. One day Vogler is ill in bed for a week. So Gustav doles out the soup. And when Vogler comes back and wants to resume his duties, Gustav takes the ladle from him and says firmly: I'm doing this now. Vogler says: No, you're not, I've done it for years.—Gustav says: Exactly, and we've all had enough.—Give me that ladle, says Vogler, or else I'll rip your ears off, you old scarecrow.—And Gustav says: You're older than I am, you ancient bat, and I tell you, if I had a name like Vogler I would keep quiet.—Now the two of them are getting into it, ragging like a couple of schoolboys until a warden comes and breaks them up. Two years later, Gustav had his accident. With his typical obstinacy, he walked over a zebra crossing when the lights were against him, and a car ran him over, and two days later he died from his injuries. There were just a dozen or so at the funeral, that's the bachelor's lot for you, but one of them placed a sprig of rosemary on the coffin and cried his eyes out, and that was Vogler.

People remain a mystery, you can read a hundred books and you'll be no closer to understanding them, that's my view, and when I was younger, I always used to think: When I'm older, I'll work it out. You see, when you're young, you see old fellows with white hair, and you think: They may be old and knackered, but they have experience of life, they're not floundering like us, and maybe they have wisdom. And suddenly you're old and gray yourself, and you realize that's all you are, old and gray and just as clueless as you ever were, and so I say: No one's got the secret. I often think we should view everything from above, we should look down on the world from way up high, and who knows what we would see, what connections, what never-guessed bridges and linkages, or then again maybe not. What a tangled mess, what a confused jumble, I don't know. Either way, we would see everything as runtish as it probably is in reality, and it might make us laugh till we cried, I don't know, all I see is persons who have already flown, and who therefore ought to know, I see them piling out of their planes and crawling off over the ground, as though it wasn't anything, a human never learns and doesn't want to learn, and just grunts on his way, isn't that right, Beth, maybe we're not totally clueless, maybe we pick up this and that, and whoever has learned something gets a bit grumpy, that's perfectly normal. I'm not bothered when Klär tells me I'm a malcontent, she looks after me and does the household. That she at the age of sixty-one still goes around singing to herself, that's her affair, she's fine, perhaps just a bit of a Holy Roller, like Gret was too. I have had occasion to observe that devout persons are cheerful. Devout people whistle in a thunderstorm, they're like that. I think they don't see much except their Almighty, and what little they do see suits them and that makes them cheerful. Klär can't put it together, she doesn't want to, she says we're God's children, which makes us good. I say: You blue-eyed optimist, you, we're the devil, we ruin and abuse God's world from dawn till dusk. Not even our lord and master would think of calling us good.—It's a matter of faith, Klär says, in the end man is good, you just need to keep telling him so.—I say: You mean yell in the ear of every Satanic capitalist exploiter: In the final analysis, you're good.—Yes, says Klär, you should.—Devout people aren't dangerous, but they can be obstinate, maybe overly mild, and because they're always grace abounding, they can be somewhat dull-witted. Gret was also devout, at least at the beginning of our marriage she was, and it took her a while to stop thinking Saturday nights were sinful and hauling me off to church on Sundays.

I'm no heathen, in my own way I believe in God and His angels, only I don't need a minister to help me, and organ-playing gives me earache. I often say to myself: God doesn't want to be promoted like shoe polish, He dislikes propaganda, He would rather we were just decent people and go easy on His creation.

All right, Beth, I reckon we're done. Every time I milk you, I think it's a miracle you're alive. It's almost six years since the morning I walked into the cowshed. Bertha is stamping and scraping, and I think, Aha, her time has come, and I put out plenty of straw for her. Then at six the gleaming white calf's hooves are sticking out of her, and I tie a string to each leg, and pull each time she pushes. No good, nothing's happening. After half an hour I go and get young Feusi, who turns off his milking machine and comes and helps me pull. We get her a couple of inches farther along, still no sign of the muzzle, but between the feet there's the purple-black tongue. Hopeless, says Feusi, I'll get more help. He comes back with Heini Gaupp. We fit a crosstie to each rope and the three of us pull. All the time, Bertha's lowing to beat the band. Finally, something gives, I sigh with relief, but no dice, it's only out up to the withers, all the rest is stuck inside, and the slimy head is dangling down, the calf is rolling its eyes and wauling in that muffled way, and Gaupp says: It's gonna die.—We go on pulling, another ten minutes, and Gaupp says: This is hopeless, I'm going to get reinforcements. He comes back with Hans Oschwald, the strongest man in the village, and the four of us pull like oxen, Bertha's wheezing, the calf is stuck fast, it's like it's caught in a vise, then one rope snaps and then the other one immediately after, all four of us are thrown against the rear wall, and

Oschwald says: These ropes must be a hundred years old. And Gaupp says: They're both going to die, cow and calf.— Just then there's a splish, and little Bethli's out in the open, I wipe you down with straw, you're a live little wriggler, well grown and solid, like a calf out of a child's encyclopedia.

9

THE EARLY birds of spring were warbling when I slid rather easily out of my mother. There wasn't much for Dorli Zolgg, the local midwife, to do, just wipe me down and check me for defects. It seemed I was intact; I was normal, they said, from the get-go. Strikingly alert as an infant, by the end of my second month I was vocalizing for hours.

In the morning I'm miserable, at night I'm scared, and during the day I am at pains not to attract attention, putting one foot in front of the other, forming sentences, combing my hair, leaving tips for the waitstaff and buying five tomatoes and answering the telephone in my best and brightest voice, reading this and that in the newspaper, not killing myself, showering regularly. And I give advice to people and listen to them and feel moved by their confidence in me. I sit around, I drink, I brood, I pat myself down for flaws and find many and each evening I say: Starting tomorrow I'm going to get a grip on myself.

I waver between conflicting feelings. One says: You need to change everything. The other says: True love transcends circumstances.

Couples counseling. The way you are, one husband (and

my client) says to his wife, I can't possibly go on loving you. —I might be different if you would love me, she replies.

That's what I mean. It gets my theologian's blood going: Chaos is waiting to be kissed by God, without the sun what's frozen stays frozen. It's as though what's neglected pricks up its ears so as not to miss the word of love. If the status quo knows how much it's hated, it will become even more hateful. A warm look, and the wallflower blossoms.

Love that transcends circumstances is not, as one might fear, conservative. After all, it doesn't conserve, it alters, thaws, makes movement and transformation possible. The de-icing beam of love gives it a revolutionary thrust.

It should all be different: It *would* perhaps all be different if you could get over yourself sufficiently for now to like it as it *is*. Courses in which tenderness is taught find plenty of take-up, though not many find it in themselves to feel sympathy when required. Here the theologian strikes again and—almost sadistically—deploys transcendence: The ability to love is grace.

Churchy, or what. Wherever reason stops to draw breath, God is whistled up. If I'm ashamed of anything in my life, it's that I too once earned my crust that way. And while I'm on feelings of shame, let me recall some of the expressions I would use on a daily basis: Risk marriage. Risk conversation. Push on to an encounter. Open your heart. To this, to that.

I ventilate.

And feel my gullet, feel the wine, I'm not up to the love theme, but it's time for the great crises of my married life. Up in

Zuzgen, Canton Aargau, I was giving a talk one winter: "The Cure of Souls in the Here and Now."—No, wrong, Zuzgen was where they held the conference of the Swiss branch of the Reformed Leprosy Mission. Anyway, be that as it may, once, in the fourth year of my marriage, I got home late for some reason or other. Helen had been in bed for hours. A note was left out for me on the lid of the lavatory, on a heart-shaped piece of paper. I felt pleased. Such things, as one may know, are what keep a marriage supple. What met my eyes was the following: "This WC has been newly scrubbed, and asks to be treated with respect." There, what does our gullet-dweller say to that? Is that tolerable? Does such an appeal not burst the bounds of what is maritally permissible? One thing, one thing only. Some eleven years later, I would not have hesitated to produce my pecker and willfully aim astray. *Puddles on the Floor* by I. P. Squint. But back then, what did I do? I betook myself to bed with full bladder, feeling crushed. I resolved to risk conversation the next morning.

It didn't happen. The girls made too much noise over breakfast, and Helen was putting pressure on me for the umpteenth time to invest in a leisure jacket. It was just conceivable that I might consider such a thing, I replied, but only if it went by another name.—You're so stubborn, came the reply, that's a detail.—I say loudly: Helen, I will have no truck with any leisure jacket!—She says: They are making some now that are machine-washable.—I'm not interested.—Oh, so it doesn't interest you whether your things are a lot of trouble to take care of or not, the pasha takes it all for granted.—Helen, you know how much I value your labor.—Oh, do you even see it? Do you understand that a toilet doesn't clean itself?—I understand that.—You never thanked me.—I thank you.

Things shouldn't be allowed to proceed to such a degree that anyone who finds fault with the state is accounted an enemy of the state. Comparably, or analogously, a mild criticism of your wife makes you a misogynist. Today it is perfectly acceptable for women to talk publicly about cutting off cocks; all we are still permitted to do is retract them. I have been working in the social professions for twenty years now. As minister and counselor, I witnessed dozens of cases of wives subtly tyrannizing their husbands. Yes, there is the crude and brutal and state-supported rule of men, no question, and I hate it. But there is as well the far discreeter subjugation of men by women, the subterranean violence, the pseudo-gentle rapine, that too is understood, but anyone who dares say so aloud is macho and a chauvinist, while anyone who blesses women, or perhaps—it comes to the same thing—continues to see them as long-suffering, which is truly to denigrate them, he is a highly modern knight and gallant spirit.

I am standing in the butcher's shop. There were three women ahead of me, and a further seven came in later. The butcher—a woman—is serving customers. After the third, she asks: Whose turn is it next?—I say: Mine.—The woman to my right says more loudly: I'd like a pound of minced steak.—Certainly! says the butcher. And then: Who's next?—I say: I am.—The woman behind me calls: Half a pound of lean bacon, and a bit of something for the dog.—Certainly, says the butcher, serves her, and asks: And who's next?—I say right away: A bratwurst!—At the same time a woman to my left says: Do you mind, I've been here far longer than you, two pounds of stewing veal.

I'm not blind.

I stroke Helen. Helen says: I'm so tired, Franz.

I stroke her. She says: I've got a headache.

She strokes me. I remain ever so slightly guarded. She says: A body could dry out next to you.

In the department store she says: Here are the socks you need.—I say: I prefer the brown ones.—Don't you think green is cheerier?—I say: I'd like the brown ones.—She says: Have it your own way, you obstinate fellow.

I loved her. I sucked peppermints before approaching her. I quit smoking. I bought the green socks, and shortly before the end of the marriage a leisure jacket as well. Almost nothing about Helen bothered me, then. She was *the* woman for me, even in the thoughtlessness of the last summer. The fact that Kezi's lips were soft beyond compare struck me as wonderful, but not decisive: I liked Helen. It's hindsight that gives me pause; in the end it's just the frog that makes me look for the disadvantages of my wife.

This is no time to give in. She *did have* disadvantages, perhaps she truly was—as Paul rather drastically put it—a sourpuss that thought it was a sugarplum.

That would be fine. I'm dying to be let off the hook. But what if it showed that I was partly to blame for Helen's drawbacks, which made my guilt understandable if not forgivable? Then I would be lost. And yet: As a psychologist, I have to ask myself that question. Whereas as Franz and as a human being, I decline a broad answer, and content myself with saying again: I could not endure differences at that time, and harmony was more important to me than the color of my socks. I ducked out of the power struggle, and in so doing perhaps made Helen still more powerful. Her will grew as mine declined (I thought it was meekness). Her domineering ways, not held in check by any table-thumping on my part, began to settle in.

Franz Milquetoast.

Please, I was naive, nothing worse than that. At the time, I still viewed marriage as a picturesque state park, an island that should be kept clear of political befouling. Most foreign to marriage, I believed at the time, was strategy and tactics. I have learned since then. Marriage—unless I'm completely mistaken—is a duel between fools, a negotiated lowering of the pants, a microcosm of the global power struggle. It pains me to see young people, fired by mendacious propaganda, run into misery like lemming hordes, only shortly afterwards to beat a path to my practice and sit in my waiting room embittered and crushed. Even bed—the last resort, one might hope, the *hortus conclusus*—is reduced to an arena, My husband comes so fast and wants me to hurry up; My wife is such a slowpoke, Jesus; He screams during intercourse, is that normal, She's so quiet during intercourse, is that normal; She scratches, He bites, Is that normal, Is that normal, Herr Thalmann?

I'm about to quit my job and quit this life too, Paul's right, almost everything is dull and bland, the only thing that's dull and good is spaghetti, says Paul.

How will I make it to dawn, with every glass the world looks more of a mess to me, last June he finally stopped his fidgeting, elderflower scent in a village graveyard, the landlady and Frau Mesmer both in tears, Paul rather perky, Myrta inscrutable, myself empty, half the village in the somber semicircle, hymns, prayers, Aunt Klär and Paul and Myrta all scattering rose petals, I scattered no rose petals, I've got his last will in my bones, "I don't want Franz over my coffin," disturbing the peace of the dead, at my father's graveside I am not yearning for reconciliation, I am yearning for Kezi's skin, a sense of triumph: I at least am still alive. And straightaway shame and renewed panic: I'm gray, almost fifty, I'm descended from him, bong, and the cell divides and grows and is named Franz, and time hisses past unapprehended, you're already looking for a caption for your life and you're thinking roughly and crudely: Dead bellend.

Death, when it didn't make my brain go blank, has always given rise to the bleakest thoughts in me. It would be possible to be cheerful if it simply destroyed life, but it's not kind enough to do that, that would mean underestimating its ambition; rather, it nullifies it, our existence. It's more than just a muscular phenomenon that all corpses have staring eyes, reflecting the horror that comes over every dying person looking back. Death takes us by the shoulder, turns us through a hundred and eighty degrees—as though dancing with us—shoves its bony knee in our crotch, and orders: Now open your eyes!—And we, used to looking forward, used to living with an aim in mind, in the belief that every forward step had a purpose, we now look in consternation at what the abrupt change of perspective shows us for perhaps the very first time: a panorama of sublime misery.

I have stood by deathbeds in my time. As a minister. And was always overtaxed, helpless, guilty. It wasn't indifference, quite the opposite, I had too keen a sense of my powerlessness, I sensed that for the dying person the comforting words he was so anxious to hear sounded pitiful, and that it's only from politeness and feebleness that he refrained from bursting out into a cackle of mockery. Inconsolableness is the ordinary feeling of the one departing, take his hand, don't say much, feel his struggle: He will feel deceived, like the racing cyclist pushing optimistically on the pedals and—lent wings by the vision of the finish, or even of victory—trampling through stage after stage. He approaches the line, he hoists his bum off the saddle and sprints, doesn't see that just behind the line the road has given way, there is a hole in the ground waiting for him, and he crashes into it. Everyone does.

Who would seek to be a cyclist if it were understood that at the end of everything is a hole in the ground? Wrong question. How explain the fact that everyone signs up and races as hard as they can, even though the true objective of so much treading has been common knowledge for eternities? A cynical question. One has no choice. Participation is compulsory. Whoever lives, pedals, end of.

I have stood by deathbeds in my time, and what I saw came in three categories. One. The destination can be seen as a gateway to our actual home. This is the technique called transfiguration. A brute fact becomes the promise of salvation, the merciless ending an opportunity. Extremity is the mother of invention, and every day pamphlets come fluttering down telling us about mute individuals released by their dying. Two. The end is usually unwelcome when it comes, but one could reach some accommodation with it if it were at the end of some other text. Therefore, rewrite. The first version transfigures the destination, the second the way there. Whoever attempts this will come to appreciate a mathematical situation. Along the vertical y axis we mark the fear of death, along the horizontal x axis the fullness of life. Both increase from zero. My contention: y is inversely proportionate to x. In other words, the graph shape is a hyperbola, slowly approaching the x, respectively the y axis. In other words, as the fullness of life grows to infinity, then the fear of death (asymptotically, admittedly) tends towards zero. Put in layman's terms: The pleasanter a life, the calmer the end. Some individuals, as I say, try to rewrite their piece, but most—this is three, coming up here—most leave that to the survivors and stare, as I say, full of dread into the mean botch that in the language of the obituaries is termed "a rich and full life."

Strange, he is hardly moving, I breathe a little more easily, but still not altogether freely, and so I continue: Anyone saying "and yet" deserves to be smacked. We live for moments, and are so utterly full of ourselves. One takes the expression "theme," the other speaks of "musical framing," a third says "demand profile," and the terms ring as though those who use them had the expectation of living forever, and I can't understand why the mouth is not accounted among the private parts. We live for moments, and obsess about our trouser creases, and if a soft-boiled egg comes out hard we make a fuss about it. There ought to be a comma here! we say. And: Isn't it high time Hürlimann pruned his hedge? I adore caraway seeds. Not my type. Natural or manmade sponge? You haven't heard the last of this. I am considering what steps to take as Swiss radio has started to fade out yodels after the third verse. Hey, is Meyer queer, he's wearing that pink sweater vest again. We live for moments and are so conceited, so gabby, so superficial-to-high-heaven, and all the time we do our doody we do our doody, and it makes us rotten and stupid and we make a din and fuck stupidly. We don't have the courage for anything, and everything frightens us. We get up early and we do our doody and feel guilty if we lie in, and wish we could claim we had a cold. We take less pleasure in escapades, even before the excess the night before we think of the rue the morning after, not only do we have less enjoyment, we enjoy our enjoyment less, it seems

almost obscene, but not renunciation and not doody and not
our incessant obedience and biddableness and their consequences, idiocy. We are so tame, so intimidated, pleasantness
takes precedence, because everything's so complicated and
so happily relative, we're excused in advance for not saying
this and not saying that, self-censorship is accounted care,
and fear of reality is tolerance, and even the most doddery
fool has a chance of being taken for a compromise-ready soul.
Is our walk relaxed? It is not. We walk, as we live, hunched,
pressed, bent, and ungainly. How do we dance? We do not
dance, at the most, we may hop. Where is there a happy face,
free from anxiety, free from pretense, free from the fear of
disapproval? Where is the evidence that could support my
hope that all my night thoughts are merely alcohol- and
frog-conditioned nightmares? Anna is dead. She had to go.
She didn't fit in. And Kezi slumbers where? Does someone
lie at her side, gazing into her face, disbelieving his own good
fortune? So or so or any old how, we live for moments and
everything withers at a dismaying pace, and the fact that my
clothes will outlive me only underlines the misery of it all,
while the bells chime brightly and the organ is as dignified
as the obituary, the worms bestir themselves, I ventilate.

And yet, a verse from the doughtiest of the prophets, a verse
from Isaiah, son of Amos.

"None calleth for justice, nor any pleadeth for truth."

A wise saying. And fits my visitor like a glove. Admittedly,
six verses later, the prophet calls for justice himself, and says
what must be said about our lives more beguilingly than any
other.

"We grope for the wall like the blind, and we grope as if

we had no eyes: we stumble at noonday as in the night; we
are in desolate places as dead men."

And otherwise? Won't it ever get light?

And Kezi slumbers where?
　　Don't look me up anymore, Franz.
　　I have to see you.
　　I feel dead inside, don't visit me anymore.
　　Not after you've done your time?
　　No, it's over.
　　She drops her head, looks along her body, avoids my eye,
she is terribly pale, where is her mouth, her lips are not loose,
nor set in some expression or other, only bleached almost
out of existence; her cheekbones prominent as ever, not jag-
ged, but smooth as they always were, and familiar too the
center parting, though the hair is hanging down in lifeless
black hanks.
　　Go now.
　　How can I live without you.
　　Go now.
　　And life goes on, you cut your nails, and dab aftershave
on your chin and wipe your spectacles, a cold won't kill you,
lumbago comes and goes, the dentist says: Rinse now.
　　And otherwise? A yearning often for humility, or burst
the bounds, sip a lager without shame and feel insistently:
Is there any happiness to match a warmed set of pajamas.
Greet the sunflower, be receptive to birdsong when ringed
by cruise missiles, sit at the edge of the thinning forest and
pass a hand over your brow.

Anna ate a fried egg sunny-side up before she passed.

But in the depths of your soul remain unreconciled, alert and hungry. Send away all who think they can feed you; whether they talk East, West, or Paradise, they don't have your best interests at heart, they are in the service of the world machine, which will behave the worse when one or two satiated individuals give it a nod.

And otherwise?

An empty mind, wind and rain. Two full ashtrays. Bulldog clips. An abusive letter on recycled paper. A glue stick and a candlestick. A corkscrew. A complete set of an encyclopedia, from A to Z. Puff pastry crumbs. A pair of paper scissors. Bottles. Matchboxes.

What else?

Receding hair and smoker's skin.

And?

And sometimes tears come to my eyes when I touch my collarbone.

10

BROWN or brindled, that is the question. For decades there have been two schools of thought in the village, two camps, the brown and the brindled. It's almost unheard of for anyone to change sides, because no one trusts a turncoat. There is a further group, the so-called colored fools, and they keep both kinds, but these mixed owners enjoy little respect, being neither fish nor fowl, and I am of their party, I keep four brown cows and one pale brindle, called Star. I could just as well own four brindles and a brown, I think the whole dispute is ridiculous, I have enough experience, I've been to dozens of cattle performance shows and animal husbandry events, I've had browns and brindles in my cowshed, and I know all there is to know about milk yields, fat content, feed quotients, and illness susceptibility, I am informed about the respective growth rates and temperaments, weight gain and slaughter yield of the two races, and the conclusion I have come to is this: There is nothing between them, one performs slightly better in one metric, the other in another, but both have their joys and sorrows, and if you're unlucky both can let you down, the thing that matters is how you rear and feed them, that's only logical, an empty sack never stands upright, and you milk a cow through her mouth. All in all, it's not that different from people, it's a question of how you treat them, a cow needs proper grass, grass needs good soil, a person needs proper warmth, otherwise you'll make him into an empty sack, a layabout, a dreamer, a fool who will believe any old crap and who will hang on the lips or tits of any preacher of doom. I tell you one thing: If you abolish human warmth because it can't be afforded, if instead of a warm nook you offer them junk and pretension and train them to look down their noses at pleasantness, then God knows you won't be surprised by our time and all the waxen images and the cold cripples in whose gaping emotional void a plastic bladder swells, filled with hate and fear and fake toughness. Fanaticism and militarism and any other form of deceit and foolishness is in the end nothing but lack of warmth, and it's not for nothing that they say of the devil that his tail—or do they mean his prick—is cold as ice. But what's the use, I'm just an old geezer, the world is as it is, and if it decides to end, then that's what it deserves to do, and no one is to try and tell me it was just the fault of a handful of lunatics. There need to be several million other lunatics gagging for a top lunatic to push the button and give the word for the steam hate vent to be opened. I dread it, just as I dread the hysteria of the press and all the other varmints East and West who have gotten by all their lives on sowing disunity, and if that seed opens, then they act all bothered, and sob fake tears, those perfidious panting dogs, I thank the Lord I'm almost eighty, please God I don't live to see that blind craziness and that whole hopeless fiendishness anymore, please God.

Many times I was almost as far along as my father, woke up with real thick disgust in me, and I took hold of Gret's hand and said: I wish they'd dashed out my brains when I was born.—Often I walked around the cowshed in the early morning and stared at the ropes and thought, Yup, I'll do it. My father did it, my brother Wendel did it, and I didn't do it, in spite of all the vileness. Often I'd feel strangely unhappy in my heart for day after day, and I'd shuffle around beat, and at night I'd crawl into bed and say to Gret: These past few nights, I've dreamed that I was a carcass.—Other than that, I didn't say much of anything, grief muted me and gummed up my tongue, I shuffled around, followed from morn till late by a voice that whined after me: You're a cursed son of Adam.—I got through it with help from Gret and from God, and I allowed myself to live, and I decided not to gallop away, but to approach the grave in the pilgrim's way that God wants us to.

My little brother did it, Wendelin at thirty-one topped himself, and left behind Ursula with a couple of nippers. I've felt the weight of a two-hundredweight sack on my neck for years now, he wrote in his farewell note, I don't know what's in it, probably a mixture of lead and sins, I'm a black plague, look after yourselves.

People were fond of Wendel, the only thing no one really understood was his fear that he was a terrible sinner. In his last year, Ursula says, he would sit at the kitchen table most evenings and read half-aloud from the newspaper, but only the parts about break-ins and accidents. He would read an article and tell her: It wasn't me, it was nothing to do with me, I've got an alibi, you can be my witness, it's really not nice coming under constant suspicion.—No one's suspecting you, Ursula replies, no one.—Yes, they are, he says, I know for a fact.—And so it went. And if someone really can't carry on, no one can stop him, affection can't reach him, he doesn't trust it, he wraps himself in fantasy, his heart freezes under sealed pores, and even the sun feels cold to him and deepens his melancholy, and I understand all that. Whether it's a grape or a roof tile, every damned thing on earth just wants to drop like cat shit, and only we humans feel under an obligation to keep pinching ourselves in the behind so that the heavy skull doesn't go crashing to the ground. I was always perplexed that someone falling is still called upon to provide justification, as opposed to someone who just jogtrots through life.

Well, it's all one to me. The world has this and that still wrong with it, but I don't care, I've got the bulk of it behind me, and no one's to say old Thalmann's clinging on to life like a blade of grass in a crusty cowpat. I just have one thing to say: I'm happy to go, but I won't go quietly, I will never make peace with this stinking hole, and when I say I don't care, I don't mean surrender either. That won't happen, not even if there are fifteen priests round my deathbed, I'm sticking to it, and I'll tell them: Do you smell that rancid reek, your world is a lump of lard, and I'm going to tell them about it upstairs.—Who knows what God will make of me anyway, I quarreled with Him often enough, and rarely understood Him, and least of all when He took Anna from me, the dear, sweet child. I've done this and that, a human life will contain a thousand bad deeds, so much impatience and so many choleric outbursts against flies and other such harmless creatures, swearing, lying, blaspheming, tormenting, mocking, sulking, deceiving, blaming, we are greedy and confused and feigning and so on and on, and in the end we are the same disgrace as any other, hoping in vain for a peaceful end. I want to be like that, I used to say when I was a little urchin, just like that man in the illustrated Bible, with a nice smile and raising his hand and blessing one and all.—But you'll never turn out like that, little Menzli, says my mother, do you even know what "blessing" is?—I reply: Yes, it's saying hello to people with a nice smile.—That too, says my mother, but it's more than that, it means to protect and love and forgive.—All at the same time? I ask. She says: Yes, Menzli, yes.

And she was right, I wasn't able to become like the man in the Bible. I don't beam at people and bless them, least of all the way things are now. I don't give a shit for wisdom. I don't give a shit about sitting on my milking stool and responding to every bit of skullduggery with a blissed-out savior's smile. Where would that get us? Where does it get us when every idiocy, every wormy head of cabbage is first tolerated, and then forgiven? Look about you, and you'll see. Read the paper. Listen to the radio. Everything is damage. Pigsty talk and reporting from the gutter, interspersed with sports. And when you sit in the Lamb and tell it like it really is, then they say: You're a gloommonger, we're here to play cards, you can keep your lectures for the cows.—And Mäder says to Feusi: Let the old billy goat low.—We have peace, says Mosimann, no one's starving, what more do you want, and as far as the forest goes, you've always had the odd dead tree, only there wasn't such a song and dance made about it.—The landlady calls out: Klemens wants to take Frau Mesmer for a walk in the woods, so he needs plenty of soft foliage!—I say: Oh, you old chook, you, and they all chime in: Makes the best soup!—And they all laugh. And they all laugh, and deal out the cards and play and drink and chew on their cigars and later on there's a bit of a singsong, landlady mine, pour the wine, or if not, beer, let's be of cheer, noses red from melancholy, so Molly Molly, lift your leg, so Hans can slip in with his peg. And then goodnight all.

I find it harder and harder. I don't go there much anymore. A story, a glass, a singsong, a cigar, and a couple of off-color jokes, God knows I don't mind, and still, as soon as I'm in bed after, I feel as scared sick as a child that's told a lie. I sleep poorly, I dream of Anna, I see her shaven skull in front of me and her dark lashes. Daddy! she cries, I'm desperate, comfort me.—I stand there crippled, and she shrivels before my eyes.

Anna. The misery of her dying weeks leached into me, for twenty-four years I've been carrying it around inside me, her death bent me double and made me impatient with all other forms of injustice. At the time I was quietly hating Gret for her submissiveness. She's wallowing in Bible verses, I thought, and gratefully kissing every hand that grabs our poor girl by the neck and shakes her to death. Anna herself also stayed devout to the end, and hardly fussed, and said: He wounds, but He also binds.—He binds nothing, and He made her suffer, she grew thinner by the day, and her hair fell out. She clearly felt the horror of her visitors, she smiled, and that smile distorted her features, and made it even harder to offer a word of comfort. She was so beautiful and fresh and August Knüsel said: Klemens, I'm not exaggerating, I taught school here for forty-three years, and I'm telling you in all that time no other child was as bright as your Anna and as clever and original.

Bright kids die young, they say, and on Twelfth Night, the sixth of January 1959, Anna had bleeding gums for a day and a night. We send her to the doctor who sends her to the hospital, and they tell us: Leukemia. What's that? we ask, they say: A disease of the blood, there's little hope.—And they treated her and she grew pale and feeble, there was less of her every day and she said: Take me home, let me stay home.—We put her on the sofa in the living room and tended her there for twelve weeks, and her blue eyes were bright and warm till her very last day, Saint Mark's, the twenty-fifth of

April. For ever and aye that was a bad day, my late father used to say: No larks on Saint Mark's.—Early in the morning she is strangely lively, and her fallen cheeks are flushed. She sits up and says to me: I feel well and I'd like a fried egg and half an onion, please.—To eat? I ask in bewilderment.—She says: Of course, little Papa, what else, today life is going to begin again.—I bring her what she wants, then I run over to the cowshed, and milk my thirteen cows, and I think: There are two possibilities, one is a miracle, the other is death at hand, please God, help her to get up, make her well, accomplish the miracle. And when I look in on the house at eight o'clock, she's still and ghostly pale on the pillows, and Gret and Myrta are huddled beside her, and stroking her hands and her brow, and her breath is coming feebly. I walk up to the couch, and Anna opens her eyes, looks at me, and asks: Is it ten already?—I say: No, it's only eight o'clock.—She sighs, and closes her eyes again. Gret says to Myrta: Send for the pastor.—I say: Bah, it's the doctor we want.—Gret whispers: Klemens, please, I can feel her slipping away.—I say: Nonsense, it's just a crisis, three hours ago she wanted her breakfast.—And Anna smiles, and says quietly: I'm a little swallow.

At nine o'clock, Pastor Boll comes along, a venerable old gentleman, somewhat stiff, a lifelong teetotaler, but otherwise pretty much on the level. In 1938 he baptized her, and in 1954 confirmed her, her Bible verse is framed and to this day hangs in the best room: "Truly the light is sweet, and a pleasant thing it is for the eyes to behold the sun." The minister goes in to see Anna, and Gret and I wait in the kitchen. Myrta stays by her bedside. Anna is awake. He talks to her, he gives her comfort. She says: I wish I could have snogged someone like mad.—He says: Let us pray.—He prays. She is fading. Anna, he asks, do you have a wish still?—She opens her eyes, thinks hard and then says loud and clear: Yes, I'd like a beer.—And Pastor Boll looks at her aghast and mutters: My dear child, you should reconsider, that will not be to the Lord's liking.—And Anna opens her eyes wide and whispers something and dies. She dies on the dot of ten.

So it goes. At the age of twenty-one she must quit this life. That was the Almighty's reward for her devoutness. He kills off the pure of heart, He letteth the sinners to run wild, I said to Gret. She looks at me, half-cross, half-sad, and replies: He's the Almighty, don't criticize His ways.—I lose control, and hiss back at her: You're damn right I criticize His ways, I shit on them, you little amen corner, you.—Then we cried together, and in the evening I dug Anna's grave, and a blackbird sang in the elderflower, and at eleven o'clock on Friday we carried our child to her place of rest.

Gret passed on four years later. Heart failure. You sleep, you wake, you get up, and you die, that's about the size of it. And actually any heart can give up the ghost at any time. Mine included. I'm seventy-nine now. It's not being afraid. I just don't get it. I say, it stands to reason, I'll kick the bucket too one day. Everyone says that, even if in every case it sounds like something they've learned to say and are being made to say. But in the end they don't really believe in it, and they can't see themselves as a corpse or a skeleton, much less as mold and dust. The head says: I know I'm going to kick off. And the feeling says: It won't happen to me, I know I won't live forever, but a while longer anyway, and then who knows.

Paul was a cemetery gardener and knew the people there and had access to the crematorium. There are peepholes, he said, where they supervise the incineration. Five thousand degrees, if I'm not mistaken, he said, the coffin is gone within four seconds, and then you see the body writhing, some even stand up, you wouldn't believe such a thing, Paul says, but they stand there, and their arms are moving as though they're conducting an orchestra, it's hell, it's unfathomable, and all the employees say: That's life.

Quiet now, Star, you should be glad it's a couple of human hands milking you and not four cold metal-and-rubber teat clamps. I'm the only one in the village who still does it the old way. When the bells sound for me, you'll be made acquainted with the machine, or else you'll be sent to the knacker's. That's the way it is now, if it takes time and trouble, forget it. Earlier they used to say: Rome wasn't built in a day, these days they swear by haste, and so the good things are dying out. It's not worth the time, they say, and that infects everything, including education, love, agriculture, you name it. They rumble around the fields on hundred-horsepower tractors, and their reaper-binders are kept going day and night, anyone who takes a breather is certain to go broke. Quickest is best, everyone knows, and nature is run raggeder by the day, everyone knows, and in the end we'll be left on a barren planet, grinning at each other in confusion, and saying: Ever and ever, amen.—And on the big gravestone you can read the inscription: Here lies the human race, we were quick about it, it saved time.

I'm not saying you should be lame and slothful like a housefly in winter. I'm just asking: At the moment your hour strikes, where is the time you've saved? Do you reckon it all up, and then present the bill upstairs? I ask: Does it feel great when you brag about having outrun the competition when you're on your deathbed? Do you think your chasing about has impressed the Lord, do you imagine the worms tucking into you will give you extra respect because you chased through life so breathlessly?

No. Man lives badly, I think almost everyone feels that, even if it's been drummed into us from birth that bad is good. A little spark of something is in anyone, only it doesn't light a beacon, there is no good wind, a cold, wet rag stifles the spark, and it throws up smoke that fogs our senses and smuts our souls. Almost everyone feels it, no one does anything about it. The wish to burn gradually shrinks, the black crust grows and becomes our place. That's the way of it. Then one day you're lying on your deathbed, and your past is a bollix, and your future a puff of dust.

All right, Star, that was it. We're still alive. I milk, you give milk, we're still among the living. I'll take it as it comes. Next, I'm off to dig manure, and at eight there's milky coffee and I'll read the paper, and sooner or later they'll be standing around me singing lustily, "O blest are those who trust in God" and thinking: There, at last, he's quit fidgeting.

OTHER NEW YORK REVIEW CLASSICS

For a complete list of titles, visit www.nyrb.com.